STORIES FROM EAST HIGH #9

RINGIN' IT IN

By N. B. Grace

Based on the Disney Channel Original Movie
"High School Musical," Written by Peter Barsocchini
Based on "High School Musical 2," Written by Peter Barsocchini
Based on Characters Created by Peter Barsocchini

Bath New York Singapore Hong Kong Cologne Delhi Melbourne

First published by Parragon in 2009
Parragon
Queen Street House
4 Queen Street
Bath BA1 1HE, UK

ISBN 978-1-4075-2508-2

Printed in UK

CHAPTER ONE

Fresh snow blanketed the Sky Mountain Ski Resort, the snowflakes sparkling in the sun. The sky was a bright, clear blue. The air was crisp and smelled like pine. It looked, Gabriella Montez thought, like a gorgeous picture postcard – and the sight of the main lodge building brought back wonderful memories of her visit last year, when she had first met Troy Bolton.

As if Troy sensed what she was thinking, he came up behind her and said into her ear, "Want to sing some karaoke tonight?" When she turned to smile at him, he added teasingly, "Or would you rather hang out by the fire and read a book?"

"No way!" She laughed. "I'm not going to spend one minute of this holiday alone when I can hang out with my friends."

Gabriella looked past him to see the other Wildcats chattering happily as they pulled their suitcases out of the cars. What a difference a year makes, she thought. This time last year, I was sad because I was moving; all I cared about was studying, and I was sure I'd never make any friends as good as the ones I left behind. And now . . . .

"Okay guys, everybody count your bags and make sure you have everything," Troy's dad, Coach Bolton, called out. "Then we'll check in and start having some fun!"

Everyone cheered. Troy's parents had come up with the idea of organizing a group trip to the ski resort that they had visited for years as family. They had talked to the other parents and, before they knew it, the winter break had become another Wildcat adventure. Mrs Montez had been glad to sign up as a chaperone, along with Mr and Mrs Bolton. After a flurry of phone calls, Chad Danforth, Sharpay and Ryan Evans, Taylor McKessie, Zeke Baylor, Jason Cross, and Kelsi Nielsen got permission to come along.

"We won't get checked in for hours at this rate," Troy said with a sigh, nodding towards Sharpay and Ryan, who were dragging luggage out of their car. Sharpay had brought nine suitcases. They were all in the colour she insisted on calling "Sharpay Pink" and were emblazoned with her initials. She was wearing a new pink ski vest, jumper, and trousers. Her brother, Ryan, stood in the driveway. He also wore new ski clothes, topped with a striped ski cap. He caught Gabriella's eye and gave her a friendly wave.

"Ryan!" Sharpay snapped. "You're supposed to be in charge of our luggage!"

"I am?" he protested.

"Really? Because when we packed the car, I distinctly remember that I had nine pieces of luggage, yet I count only eight . . . ."

"Okay, wait." He dived inside onto the backseat and emerged a few seconds later holding a small vanity case. "Here you go."

She nodded regally. "Very good. Now let's check in and see what kind of upgrade we can get. I expect the Presidential Suite at the very *least*."

"I don't know about that, Sharpay," Chad said, as he walked over. "Isn't the Presidential Suite reserved for, you know, the president?" he asked, rolling his eyes.

Sharpay tossed her head. "Or someone *equally* as important," she said pointedly.

Hearing that, Taylor sighed loudly and carried her suitcase over to where Gabriella and Troy were talking with Kelsi.

"This was a great idea your parents had," Kelsi was telling Troy. "It'll be so much fun to ring in the New Year in the mountains."

"Don't forget four days of hitting the slopes," Jason added.

"That powder looks great," Zeke agreed. He had a snowboard tucked under one arm and an expression of eager anticipation on his face.

"I didn't know you cared about any powder that wasn't sugared," Chad joked. Zeke's love of baking had recently led him to an intense month of learning everything he could about making doughnuts.

"Hey, I like to get out of the kitchen once in a while," Zeke said. "In fact, I plan to pull off a 360 on this trip!"

"And I'm going for a backside 720!" Jason exclaimed. "I got close last winter. I'm sure I'll nail it this time. Come on, Chad! We can hit the slopes this afternoon if we get a move on."

"Oh, yeah, that would be great," Chad said, a little too heartily. Then he glanced at the sky and added, "But I don't think we'll have time today. It'll be dark pretty soon, and the sky looks like it's clouding up. We may be in for a storm. . . ."

Gabriella glanced at Chad curiously. He was usually the first one to get started on any kind of sports activity. She was surprised to hear him sounding so hesitant.

Troy peered at the sky. "Oh, come on, it's still light out," he said. "If we hurry, we could probably get in at least an hour on the mountain. And the clouds don't look *that* bad."

A young man standing nearby overheard their conversation. He had dark hair and bright blue eyes, and was wearing a Sky Mountain Ski Resort jacket. He strolled over to introduce himself. "Hi, guys," he said. "I'm Matt Hudson."

Before anyone could reply, Sharpay came running over. "Well, hi," she cooed. "My name is Sharpay. It's great to meet you! Have you stayed here before?"

"Well, yeah." Matt grinned. "Actually, I work here," he said. "I'm a member of the ski rescue team. Have to pay my way through college somehow."

"Really!" Sharpay seemed, if anything, even

more interested after hearing this news. "The ski *rescue* team? That sounds very heroic. *And* dangerous."

"Yeah, talk about a cool job," Zeke said, a note of envy in his voice.

"Well, it's not dangerous if you know what you're doing," Matt replied.

"Do you have to rescue a lot of people?" Kelsi asked.

"It depends," Matt said. "Sometimes we'll see a lot of action, but other times are pretty quiet. A big part of the job is letting people know how to stay safe and warning them about bad weather. That's why I wanted to talk to you guys. I know you just arrived, so you probably haven't heard about the storm we're tracking. It's supposed to come in tonight, so we're telling people not to go on the slopes until tomorrow."

"Oh, too bad," Chad commented. "I was really looking forward to trying out some new moves."

Gabriella shot him another curious look. Chad didn't sound disappointed at all. In fact, he

7

sounded relieved. Zeke and Jason looked a little crestfallen, but Troy just shrugged. "Better safe than sorry. Anyway, there's tons of other stuff to do today. Skating, video games, listening to music in the teen club – and, of course, there's always basketball!"

Chad brightened when reminded that the ski resort also had a state-of-the-art basketball court. "Great idea, captain!" he called out, as Jason gave Zeke a high five.

Taylor rolled her eyes at Gabriella and Kelsi. "You'd think they'd get tired of basketball at some point," she whispered.

"Never," Gabriella responded with a grin. "That would be like you or me getting tired of going to the library!"

"Or me getting tired of playing the piano," Kelsi added with a shy smile.

"You guys have fun," Matt said. "And if you need any information about the best spots for boarding, let me know. I spend most of my free time on the mountain."

"Thanks," Troy replied. "That sounds great."

As Matt walked away, Sharpay stared after him. "He seems nice. And *totally* cute," she said. Her gaze wandered over to Troy, then shifted to Gabriella. She added, in a sugary-sweet voice, "Don't you think so, Gabriella?"

Gabriella hesitated. She didn't want to get caught in a conversation with Sharpay about other boys and how cute they were – especially not with Troy standing within earshot!

"Well . . ." she began slowly.

She had no idea what she was going to say next, but thankfully, her mother walked over and rescued her from the awkward moment. "If you girls have all your stuff," Mrs Montez said with a smile, "I think we should get checked in."

Sharpay remained outside, bossing Ryan around and telling him how to stack her luggage as they entered the reception, while Gabriella, Taylor, and Kelsi walked through the lodge's main doors, followed by most of the other

Wildcats. Immediately, the three girls noticed a huge sign on an easel.

NEW YEAR'S EVE KARAOKE CONTEST! it announced in huge, glittering letters. SIGN UP NOW!

"Hey, Gabriella," Taylor called out, a teasing note in her voice. "That contest looks like it was designed with you and Troy in mind!"

Gabriella smiled. Everyone knew that she and Troy had first met on New Year's Eve last year at this very resort. They had been pushed into performing together in a karaoke contest and had discovered a love of singing – and quickly hit it off. It had been a magical night, and Gabriella had been thinking about nothing else since this trip had been planned. But in all the bustle of getting ready for the trip, she and Troy hadn't had a chance to spend much time together.

She glanced over at Troy, who was still talking excitedly with Chad, Zeke, and Jason about all the cool stuff there was to do at the resort. Skiing, snowboarding, skating, playing basketball on the indoor court, or swimming in the Olympic-size pool. Listening to music in the teens-only club, maybe spending an hour or two in the video game room. . . . The one thing he *wasn't* talking about was getting on a stage and singing with her.

Oh, well, Gabriella thought. Last year, we were both alone when we went to that New Year's party. This year is different. We're here with all our friends. Of course it's not going to be the same. And last year was so special, maybe it would just be better to not try to duplicate it . . . .

"Oh, I don't know about entering that contest," Gabriella said, trying to sound casual about the prospect. "You know how nervous I get in front of an audience."

Taylor lifted one eyebrow. "I think you've got over that little problem," she commented.

"I'd say so, too," Kelsi agreed. "What with starring in the school musical and everything."

Gabriella laughed at that, but shook her head. "No," she said. "I want to relax and have fun while we're here, not worry about a singing contest."

At that moment, Sharpay flounced up to them. "Where are the bellboys?" she demanded. "And the valets? And the person who is supposed to whisk us through the check-in line?"

"I think the valets are kind of busy," Gabriella said, nodding towards a large group of teens who had arrived in a bus just before them. "I'm just going to carry my own bag. It'll be faster."

Sharpay gave Gabriella's one small suitcase a disdainful glance. "Yes, it's easy to move quickly when you bring limited wardrobe options," she sniffed. "I, of course, feel a responsibility to my fans to *always* be dressed in the latest fashions. And I never wear anything more than once on holiday. Otherwise, it's just too boring."

"Then I guess you're stuck here until someone's free to cart all your fashionable clothes to your room," Taylor said sweetly. She picked up her bag and slung it over her shoulder. "See you in a few hours, Sharpay."

Frowning, Sharpay opened her mouth to respond, but, as Taylor began to walk away, Sharpay caught sight of the karaoke contest sign. "What's this?" Her eyes gleamed with delight. "A singing contest? How perfect! Ryan!" She glanced across the foyer and saw Ryan talking to a pretty girl. They were both smiling and laughing. Sharpay raised her voice. "Ryan!"

He kept talking to the girl, who had long brown hair and sparkling brown eyes. It looked like neither of them had heard Sharpay.

"Ryan!" Sharpay yelled.

"Huh? What?" He turned around and spotted his sister, who was storming over to him. The vague expression on his face turned to one of alarm. "Oh, hi, Sharpay, look who I met! Her name is Savannah Charles. She's here with her school's ski club, and we were just talking about—"

"Yes, yes, yes, that's all very nice, I'm sure," Sharpay said briskly. "But did you see the sign about the karaoke contest?" She pointed to the sign with a grand gesture. "We should definitely enter! I know we could win. After all, most people who sing karaoke are complete amateurs who just goof around on stage. *We*, on the other hand, are consummate professionals! We would completely annihilate the competition!"

Ryan glanced at Savannah, who seemed taken aback by Sharpay's words. His sister *did* sound a bit ruthless, he admitted to himself. Not to mention competitive. But that was just Sharpay. . . .

"Savannah, this is my sister, Sharpay," he said quickly. "We're both kind of into per-forming. . . ."

"Kind of?" Sharpay was astonished. "*Kind of*?" She turned to Savannah to set the record straight. "Ryan and I live to perform," she said dramatically.

"Oh, well, that's good, I guess," Savannah remarked. "That sounds like fun."

Sharpay's eyes narrowed. "Oh, well, if you just want to have fun, I'd suggest you find someone else to sing with," she said haughtily. "Ryan and I aren't interested in *fun*–"

"We're not?" he asked.

Sharpay ignored him. "*We*," she continued, "are interested in winning."

Taylor, Kelsi, and Gabriella watched from across the room as Sharpay grabbed Ryan and pulled him over to help carry her suitcases. He managed a small goodbye wave at Savannah, who smiled sympathetically before turning back to her friends.

"Sharpay just can't stand not being the centre of attention," Taylor said, shaking her head.

"I know," Gabriella grinned. "Lucky for her, she always manages to find a spotlight!"

CHAPTER TWO

"**H**ey, guys, are you ready to hit the slopes?" Troy asked eagerly. The Wildcats had barely finished breakfast the next morning, but Troy already had on his ski jacket and knit hat. His lift ticket was hanging around his neck and he was carrying his snowboard. "It looks like a great day to be on the mountain!"

Gabriella took one last bite of toast as she looked out the window. The sky was blue and the sunshine glistened on the snow. "We're so

16

lucky that the storm ended during the night," she said with a smile. "The weather is perfect!"

"So, you're ready to try a little boarding?" Troy asked with a grin. Gabriella had never been on a snowboard in her life, and he had promised to show her the ropes.

"You bet!" Gabriella exclaimed.

"Yeah," Zeke agreed. "So let's get going!"

Jason nodded. "If we hurry, we can beat the crowd at the rental shop," he said.

At that moment, Sharpay sauntered in, dressed from head to toe in a bright-pink ski outfit and furry ski boots, holding a pair of skis and poles. She was followed by Ryan, who wore a blue ski suit and a striped hat. He also carried a pair of skis and poles.

Sharpay smirked as she overheard Jason's comment. "Oh, that's right," she said. "Some of you don't own your own gear. Fortunately, Ryan and I go skiing every year, so we always have the latest equipment." She smiled sweetly at Troy. "Except for Troy, of course. Maybe you and I could go ahead and get on the lift line? Since we don't have to wait around at the rental shop or anything . . . ."

Troy couldn't help but grin. Sharpay was always so obvious about trying to spend time alone with him! You'd think she would have worked out that I'm not interested after last summer, he thought. Working at the Lava Springs Country Club hadn't been easy, especially with Sharpay using every angle she could to snare him. Still, it had all worked out in the end and they had had a lot of fun . . . and he was determined to make sure the same thing happened on this holiday.

"That's a nice offer, Sharpay," he said politely. "But I wanted to help Gabriella pick out the right snowboard."

Sharpay's face clouded over briefly, but she quickly recovered. "Oh," she said with a huff. "Well, whatever."

"Why don't you wait for us?" Gabriella suggested. "Then we can all go to the lifts together."

Before Sharpay could respond, Chad suddenly

chimed in, "Um, actually, I think I'm going to have to pass. . . ."

"What?" Troy said, surprised. "You're not going to board with us?"

"It's my ankle," Chad explained. "I think I twisted it last night at the ice rink. You know, when I fell and slammed into the boards?"

"You seemed all right, though," Troy said. "You shook it off."

"I thought I did, too." Chad shook his head mournfully. "But I guess I was just fooling myself. It really hurts this morning." He stood up and limped to the window to demonstrate.

"That's too bad," Gabriella said. She could see that Troy was disappointed. "But you might make it worse if you tried to go out today."

"That's what I thought," Chad replied quickly.

Troy nodded. "At least you can walk. You'll probably be okay by tomorrow," he said, clearly hoping that would be the case. "You should keep your foot elevated and put ice on your ankle and—"

"Uh, yeah," Chad said, not meeting Troy's eyes. "I'll do all that, for sure."

"Well, you shouldn't have to stay here all by yourself," Taylor said casually. "The snow is pretty, but it sure looks cold. I wouldn't mind hanging out by the fire for a few hours."

"Really?" Chad looked shocked.

Glancing around at her friends, Gabriella saw that everyone's faces looked as surprised as Chad's. True, Taylor and Chad had been hanging out off and on, but Taylor always acted so cool, as if she was willing to spend time with Chad but wasn't going to go out of her way to do it. In fact, she usually gave Chad a hard time, and he usually teased her right back.

Maybe, Gabriella thought, Taylor's finally decided to ease up on Chad. And, as she watched the smile slowly spreading across his face, she added to herself, perhaps Chad will know enough to take Taylor up on her offer!

Sharpay stood in the ski-lift line, well aware of

her appearance. She had awakened before dawn to visit the resort's salon and had got her hair and make-up done; she had donned her very best ski outfit (the one that made her look like a serious, yet very fashionable, Olympic skier); and she was standing in a spot where she would be seen by everyone walking past. With the mountains behind her, she looked just like she should be on the cover of a travel magazine.

Which made it all the more annoying that no one seemed to be paying attention to her! Troy and Gabriella walked by, their heads bent towards each other, laughing. Zeke and Jason were joking with Kelsi, who was blushing but seemed to be enjoying the teasing. Even Ryan, who could always be counted on to boost her spirits with a few extravagant compliments, was nowhere to be found.

Then she spotted Matt, the absolutely gorgeous ski-rescue guy, walking towards her. Sharpay gave him a brilliant smile, then glanced at Troy to see if he had spotted his competition.

A surge of irritation swept through her when she saw that Troy was, as usual, completely oblivious. Really, he had no chance of winning her affections if he didn't start paying more attention to her!

She cleared her throat and called out, "Hi, Matt! How wonderful to see you again!"

"Huh?" Matt gave her a puzzled look, almost as if he didn't recognize her. Then his face cleared and he said, "Oh, right. You're the girl with all the luggage."

"Right!" Sharpay cried happily. Of course he remembered her! How could he forget? She was clearly the only person who cared enough about the way she looked to arrive with three outfits for each day. "I'd love to get your advice about which trails I should take," she went on, pitching her voice so that Troy would be sure to hear it. "After all, I've never been to this resort before, and you are *obviously* an expert on the mountain!"

"Uh, sure." Matt looked a little confused.

"Well, I'd suggest the Grand Prix trail, or the Mackle. They'll be challenging, but not so much so that you don't have fun."

"That sounds *wonderful*, thank you *so* much," Sharpay said in a breathy voice. "I don't suppose you'd be willing to go with me on my first run? Just to make sure I can handle it?"

"Sorry," he said politely. "I'm working right now."

"Of course." She gave him an understanding smile. "Some other time, then."

"Yeah, maybe," he shrugged. "See you around."

Satisfied that she had made her point to Troy, Sharpay flipped her hair to the side and looked over in Troy's direction. Gabriella was, as usual, droning on about how this was her very first time snowboarding and acting as if she wouldn't be able to do a thing without Troy's help.

"Do you think I can handle this?" she asked Troy for what Sharpay was sure was the hundredth time. "I won't hurt myself?"

23

"You'll be fine!" he laughed. "Remember, you've got a great teacher."

She opened her eyes wide, feigning surprise. "Oh, who's that?"

"Me, of course!" he answered, pretending to frown.

"Oh, *pul-lease!*" Sharpay exclaimed, rolling her eyes. "Are you guys finished?"

Gabriella blushed. Troy turned around, as Sharpay had hoped, and gave her a smile. Not a very big smile, Sharpay noticed, but then he was probably tired after reassuring Gabriella for the last hour.

"Those are cool skis," Troy commented to Sharpay. "I think I saw them in a magazine recently."

"Yes, they're the very latest. And, of course, they're the top of the line." Sharpay preened a little. "My father believes in buying only the best. The best skis, the best goggles, the best boots–"

"That's great, but some of us want a chance

to actually *use* our skis today," an older man behind her interrupted. "And this is the line for double lifts. If you're on your own, you need to go" –he nodded towards another line of people– "over there."

Sharpay looked around. Sure enough, Troy was standing in line with Gabriella, and Jason was with Kelsi, and Zeke was with. . . .

She suddenly realized that Zeke was giving her a hopeful smile. "You can ride on the lift with me, Sharpay," he said eagerly. "I don't have a partner yet. . . ."

Sharpay hesitated. If she went on the lift with Zeke, they might be viewed as a couple. True, Zeke baked incredible cookies, which *was* a fabulous talent. And true, he obviously liked her a lot, and it *was* nice to be adored. . . .

But if everyone thought they were a couple, then certain other boys might decide she was unattainable. Certain other boys like Troy. He might resign himself to dating Gabriella until graduation, or even longer!

Sharpay made up her mind. She had to keep Troy's hopes alive a little longer. She gave Zeke a weak smile and said, "Thanks, but I think I'll go with Ryan. I'm sure he's waiting to join me, and we have so much to discuss. You know, we're going to enter the karaoke contest as a duet and . . ."

She looked around, suddenly stopping in midsentence. She had just spotted Ryan. He was standing by the line of single riders – and chatting happily to that Savannah girl he had met yesterday! Sharpay's eyes narrowed. The nerve of him, she thought. How dare he go his own way, not even checking to see if I needed him! And that Savannah was bad news, Sharpay could tell. She was going to distract Ryan and make him lose focus. Their planned duet would turn into an absolute disaster! It was too horrible to think about. Sharpay stomped over to where Ryan was standing and grabbed his arm. "Ryan, I need to talk to you!" she demanded. *"Now!"*

"What?" Her brother's bright blue eyes were

expressing dismay. "Savannah and I were going to ride the ski lift together and have some hot chocolate when we get to the top—"

"Lovely," Sharpay snapped. "You can pencil it in for tomorrow." She dragged him off to the end of the doubles' line.

"I was having a good time talking to Savannah," Ryan protested, after they waited in line and sat down on the lift chair. They started to ascend the mountain.

"You can talk to her later," Sharpay said dismissively. "We need to go over all the details of our performance on New Year's Eve."

"Performance? Sharpay, relax! It's only karaoke!" her brother exclaimed.

"Maybe everyone else thinks it's 'only' karaoke," she said sternly, "but that's where we will show them how wrong they are! Now, I've already picked out a great song for us; it's very upbeat, so we can even throw in a few moves to sell it to the crowd. I talked to Sammy Gray, the guy who runs the karaoke machine in the teen club, and he agreed to open the club this afternoon so we can get in some private rehearsal time and plan out our routine. And I called Mother and told her to ship three or four costume choices for us. They'll arrive tomorrow, so we should figure out a time to try them on, see what works best with our number, maybe get some alterations done if necessary–"

The ski lift arrived at the mountaintop and Sharpay hoisted herself off, still talking rapidly. Ryan trailed along behind her as she glided over to where a group of skiers were getting ready for their first run.

"That sounds great," Ryan finally interrupted. "Except, um, when will we have time to, you know . . . have some fun?"

Sharpay straightened up from adjusting her skis and frowned at him. "What do you mean?" she asked. "Don't you have fun singing?"

"Well, yes," Ryan admitted. "But–"

"Don't you have fun performing on stage?" she continued.

"Of course, but–"

"And don't you have fun *winning*?" she finished triumphantly.

Ryan sighed. "Sure, sis. Whatever you say."

"Then that's that," she said crisply. "We have time for one run down the mountain. Sammy said that he'd open the club for us, even though no one's ever asked him before–"

"Because that's when everyone else is outside, having fun," Ryan muttered, but it was soft enough so that Sharpay didn't hear him.

"–so our rehearsals will be completely private," she finished. "It will be just perfect! Now, let's go!"

As Sharpay and Ryan swooshed down the mountain, they passed Troy, Gabriella, Jason, Zeke, and Kelsi, who were trying out their snowboards. Even as Ryan whizzed past, he noticed that they were falling all over the place – but they were also laughing a lot.

As for Sharpay, she managed to make a turn so that she skied right by Troy. Her form was perfect, and he would have been quite impressed if he had seen her . . . but he happened to be helping Gabriella up out of the snow at just that moment.

That's okay, she told herself, feeling happier now that she was about to set her plan in motion to win the karaoke contest. Once I get on that stage, Sharpay thought with determination, Troy won't be able to ignore me!

CHAPTER THREE

"Thanks for spending so much time teaching me how to snowboard," Gabriella told Troy later that afternoon. "I had a blast, even though I spent most of the time falling down."

"You did great," he said reassuringly. "Pretty soon, you'll be doing 360s!"

She laughed. "Somehow I doubt that, but thanks for the encouragement."

"Anytime." Troy smiled. He glanced over at the fireplace, where Chad and Taylor were sitting. "Hey, Chad and Taylor look pretty cosy, don't you think?"

"I noticed that, too." Gabriella smiled. "Do you think they planned to have a few hours alone together?"

"Well, it's hard to believe that Chad didn't want to snowboard with us," Troy said. "And that sprained ankle excuse sounded pretty lame. No pun intended." He laughed at his own joke.

Gabriella rolled her eyes. "Taylor sounded pretty eager to sit by the fire. I wonder if she's starting to realize what a catch Chad is."

"A catch?" Troy pretended to be amazed by this thought. "*Chad*?"

"Well, he is," she insisted. "Although their alone time is obviously now over."

She and Troy glanced over at the group by the fireplace. After they had come inside, Jason, Zeke, and Kelsi had joined Chad and Taylor. Now, all five were finishing what had clearly been a hard-fought board game.

"Yeah, well, maybe that's a good thing," Troy

said. "After all, we came here to have fun as a group, right? It would mess everything up if Chad and Taylor were going off on their own all the time."

Gabriella frowned slightly. "I don't know about that. . . . I mean, yeah, it's fun for us to all hang out together. But this is a very special place, Troy . . ."

"Hmm?" Troy turned to look at her. "Oh, sure, I know. You're right. I just wanted all of us to have fun together, the way we did over the summer when we were working at the country club."

"Oh. Right." Gabriella did her best to smile and hide her disappointment. All she had been thinking about for the last month was last New Year's Eve, when she had first met Troy. It was their anniversary, in a way. And even though she loved all of their friends, well . . . didn't he want to spend a *little* bit of time just with her?

Troy grabbed her hand. "Come on. Let's see what the other guys want to do now."

Apparently not. Gabriella sighed and let herself be pulled over to the group by the fire, trying to look cheerful when she was feeling anything but. Chad was jokingly pretending to protest the results of the board game, which apparently had not been in his favour.

"All I'm saying is that if I hadn't lost that turn, I'd be celebrating my victory right now," Chad complained, as Troy and Gabriella walked up to them. "I was brought down by one bad roll of the dice!"

"*And* by my superior game skills," Taylor added smugly. "This game demands logical reasoning and superior strategy. Face it, Chad, you were doomed from the start."

He grinned at her. "All the more reason why you have to be my partner next time," he said.

"Partner? This game pits one person against another in a battle to the end!" Taylor exclaimed. "The rules don't allow for partners."

"But rules are made to be broken," Troy chimed in.

"Or amended," Gabriella said with a smile. "I think choosing partners sounds like fun. Do you guys want to play another game?"

"Sure," Chad said. "I'm totally going to win this time!"

"I'm in," Taylor said, and Jason and Zeke nodded as well. But Gabriella noticed Kelsi didn't say anything. As usual, she was sitting towards the edge of the group. She always seemed content to be quiet and listen to the others joke and laugh, but now Gabriella sensed that her idea of pairing everyone up might have made Kelsi feel left out.

Before she could say anything, Kelsi stood up. "I'd love to, but I happened to see a piano in the lounge–"

"Music is calling her away from us!" Jason said dramatically.

Kelsi bit her lip. "I'm sorry, I don't mean to be rude–"

"You're not being rude! Playing music makes you happy, so you should do it," Troy said with a grin. Kelsi gave Troy a shy smile.

"But we won't have as much fun if you're not here," Gabriella protested. "Tell you what – let's postpone the board game until after dinner, when you can join us." She caught Taylor's eye and knew that she had also picked up on Kelsi's hesitation.

"Good idea," Taylor said. "Plus, I feel like checking out the sauna. You know, just relaxing, kicking back, having some girl talk. Kelsi, why don't you join us when you're finished practising?"

"Great!" Kelsi exclaimed, beaming.

"Well, I think I've had enough cold weather for one day," Troy announced. "What do you say, guys . . . should we check out the basketball court? We don't want our moves to get stale over the winter break."

"Not when we have a big game with West High next month," Zeke agreed.

Chad jumped up from the sofa. "I'm in!" he exclaimed. He pointed at Troy. "And you, my man, are going to have to work triple hard to keep up!"

"You're on!" Troy laughed.

As they all hustled out of the room, Gabriella noticed that Chad's limp seemed to have suddenly disappeared. Smiling to herself, she thought that there was definitely a hidden story there. And this afternoon, she'd make sure Taylor spilled the whole thing.

Chad was as good as his word. As soon as they hit the basketball court, he was playing as hard as if it was a championship game. He was teamed up with Jason, while Troy was paired with Zeke. The boys felt right at home on the court.

When Troy tried to go left, Chad was right there waiting for him. When he tried to shoot a layup early in the game, Chad managed to grab the ball in midair, race halfway down the court, and then score a basket. When Troy later tried to head down court, Chad was again in his way; when he tried to dodge and break his friend's tough defense, he still found his way blocked. Chad was unstoppable!

Finally, Troy held up one hand and called for a break. "Let's take five, guys," he said. "I don't know about the rest of you, but I could definitely use a drink of water."

"Not to mention the chance to take a breath," Jason added on his way to the water fountain.

Troy leaned over, his hands on his knees, panting. "You're on fire today, Chad!"

Chad shrugged modestly, but looked pleased. "I guess I just have a lot of excess energy to burn," he said. "Sitting inside, cooped up all day—"

Troy straightened up and gave him a direct look. "Yeah, I've been meaning to ask you about that. Your ankle seems a lot better now."

"Yeah, well . . ." Chad looked embarrassed.

"Come on, dude, you can tell me the truth," Troy said teasingly. "Did you and Taylor decide you would come up with an excuse to stay inside together?"

"What?" Chad said, shocked. "No! Okay, I

was kind of exaggerating how bad my ankle felt, but I had no idea Taylor would decide to hang out at the lodge, too."

Troy gave him a disbelieving glance. "Right. So, tell me again why you kept limping around and moaning about your ankle if it wasn't really hurt?" He chuckled softly.

Chad's face turned bright red. He glanced over his shoulder to see where Zeke and Jason were. They were standing by the water fountain, joking around and tossing the basketball back and forth. He turned back to Troy. "Okay, here's the thing . . ." He stopped in midsentence.

"Yeah?" Troy asked encouragingly.

"It's kind of embarrassing," Chad admitted. "I mean, I'm supposed to be an athlete, right? And a cool guy, you know? Hip, in the know . . ." He trailed off.

"Of course," Troy agreed, laughing. "So?"

"But I'm a terrible snowboarder!" Chad blurted out.

Troy's mouth dropped open in surprise. "And that's why you wouldn't come out with us today? Because you thought you might look bad?"

"No, man, because I *knew* I would look bad!" Chad threw his hands in the air in frustration. "I've tried it before, and every time I just end up doing face-plants into the snow. I'm terrible!"

Troy shook his head, still puzzled. "But we're just having fun," he pointed out. "No one's really that good. We just goof around and stuff."

Chad gave him a knowing look. "Come on, Troy," he said. "I bet you're excellent. Right?"

"Um, well, I'm okay," Troy said sheepishly. He remembered the first time he had tried to snowboard. He'd fallen a lot, but by the end of the day he had got the hang of it. From then on, he headed out to the slopes as often as he could.

"That's what I thought," Chad said. "That's why you couldn't wait to get on the mountain this morning."

Troy's face burned. Was Chad saying he was a show-off? "That's not it at all!" he protested. "I just really love to snowboard!"

"I bet you wouldn't love it so much if you looked like an idiot every time you got on a board," Chad said glumly.

Troy opened his mouth to respond, but then he had a thought. Maybe Chad was right. How often did he try something, find out he wasn't good at it, and then give up? The memory of trombone lessons, model-car kits, and a tennis racket now stuck in the back of his cupboard flooded his mind.

"Maybe not," he admitted. "But I still think you should give it another try. I promise you won't look like an idiot."

"Yeah?" Chad's voice was sceptical. "Why is that?"

"Because I'm going to teach you myself," Troy said. "I can't leave my best buddy sitting by the fireplace for the rest of our holiday!"

* * *

Back in the lodge, Taylor and Gabriella had just finished working out in the gym and were now relaxing in the sauna.

"So, Taylor," Gabriella said casually, "did you enjoy your morning?"

"Sure. Wow, it's like an oven in here, isn't it?" Taylor said, fanning herself.

Gabriella decided to get right to the point. "Come on, Taylor, I thought you wanted to talk," Gabriella complained. "You gave me that look—"

"What look?"

"*You* know. *This* one." Gabriella mimicked her meaningful glance so perfectly that Taylor had to laugh.

"Okay, you're right," she admitted. "I did have something I wanted to tell you. . . ."

"I knew it! And it's about Chad, right?" Gabriella said knowingly.

"Chad?" Taylor looked confused. "No! It's about skiing."

"What?" Now it was Gabriella's turn to look puzzled. "What are you talking about?"

Taylor sighed and mopped off her forehead with her towel. "The truth is, I shouldn't have said I'd come on this holiday."

"But it wouldn't have been any fun without you!" Gabriella cried.

"Thanks," Taylor said, smiling. "That's why I decided to come, because I knew I would miss you guys. But we're at a ski resort. Where the whole point is to go up on the mountain and ski or snowboard or do belly flops on the snow – whatever. And I can't do it!"

Gabriella looked at her friend and smiled sympathetically. "Is that all?"

Taylor frowned slightly. "It's a huge problem!" she insisted.

"No, it's not! You should have seen me today!" Gabriella exclaimed. "I was beyond horrible! But it didn't matter, because we were all laughing so much. And everybody fell down a few times, even Troy. Really, Taylor, you have to come out with us tomorrow. You'll have a great time, even if you can't snowboard."

"That's not the problem!" Taylor exclaimed. "The problem is that I'm afraid to get on the ski lift!" She put her head in her hands. "And if I can't get on the ski lift, how will I ever get to ski down the mountain?"

Gabriella looked at Taylor earnestly. "Don't worry, Taylor," she said encouragingly. "I'll help you. By the end of this trip, you'll be riding the ski lift like a pro!"

CHAPTER FOUR

The next morning, Troy and Gabriella went down to the restaurant in the ski lodge early to grab breakfast and go over their strategies. They were determined to convince Chad and Taylor to join them on the slopes. They hadn't even had their first bite of cereal, however, before Sharpay rushed in, carrying an armful of clothes.

"Where's Ryan?" she cried. "Our costumes just came in and I want him to help me decide which one will make me look the most fabulous. Oh, and to try on his own costume, too, of course."

"Costumes? For what?" Gabriella asked.

"For the karaoke contest, of course!" Sharpay rolled her eyes at how obvious this answer was. "I had Mother express-ship a selection from my wardrobe." She dropped the clothes onto a chair.

There were a number of frilly dresses in bright pink, turquoise, lemon yellow, lime green, and pearly white. They were made of satin and taffeta and decorated with hundreds of sparkles and sequins. Sharpay sighed as she looked them over. "I can't decide which one I should wear."

Zeke overheard Sharpay from his spot in the buffet line. "I don't think it really matters," he said sincerely. "You'll look great no matter which one you pick."

Sharpay sighed impatiently. "Well, of *course* I'll look fantastic, but I have to try to get inside the judges' heads. You know, sometimes the difference between winning and losing is having a good costume or a *spectacular* one!"

"It's just a karaoke contest," Troy reminded

her gently. "I wouldn't stress out too much about it if I were you."

Sharpay gave him a bright smile. "Oh, Troy, you're so thoughtful to try to calm my nerves! But you know me – the pressure of performing always brings out my best!" She gave Gabriella a narrow glance, then asked, "What about you, Gabriella? Are you planning to enter?"

Gabriella bit her lip. She had been planning to bring the subject of the karaoke contest up to Troy later that day. Casually, of course, as if it were no big deal, because of course it wasn't. Still, *she* had wanted to choose the moment when she mentioned it to Troy.

She took a deep breath. "Well, I'm not sure," she began, glancing shyly at Troy. "I guess it depends–"

Before she could finish her sentence, Sharpay added, "Of course, I know how nervous you get on stage." Then she turned her attention to Troy. "Troy, you should really enter! You have so much natural talent."

He laughed nervously. "I don't know about that," he said.

"Don't be modest! You have a great voice!" she insisted. "It just needs to be developed a bit more–"

Troy tried to interrupt her. "I keep telling you, singing's just something I do for fun–"

"–which, of course, I'd be glad to help you with," she interjected sweetly, not even listening to what he was saying. "I've booked some private rehearsal time this afternoon if you're interested . . ."

"That's really nice of you, Sharpay," Troy said. "But I think it's too nice of a day to stay inside, don't you?"

Chad leaned over and muttered to Jason and Zeke, "Stand by, guys. We may need to carry out a rescue operation for our good friend Troy."

Sharpay spun around, her gaze intense. She hadn't quite heard what Chad had said, but she could tell from the way the three of them were snickering that he was teasing her. Again.

"Some of us are devoted to our art," she huffed. "And others are devoted to juvenile humour." She turned back to Troy and continued wheedling. "You, for example, have worked hard at basketball for years. True, basketball isn't art, but still . . . look at how that paid off! Just think what you could do if you put that much time into singing!"

"Well, thanks," Troy replied. "But I kind of assumed that Gabriella and I would be singing together." He turned to smile at her. "Was I right?"

"Of course!" Gabriella exclaimed, her face glowing. "I mean, if *you* want to–"

"Absolutely," he said. "That's settled, then."

Sharpay crossed her arms and scowled at Troy and Gabriella. "Fine," she said haughtily. "But you can forget about winning the prize this year. You don't have a chance now that Ryan and I are entering!"

"Speaking of which," Chad said innocently, "where *is* Ryan, anyway?"

49

"I think I saw him with that girl he met," Jason added helpfully. "They were headed for the ski lift."

"What?" Sharpay's eyes widened. "I knew it! That girl is totally distracting him from his professional goals! I've got to go find him, right now!" She stomped away.

Chad rolled his eyes. "I hope Ryan's covered his tracks," he said. "And I mean covered them *really, really* well."

Laughing, they all headed outside.

"I have a bad feeling about this," Taylor confided to Gabriella as she stood in line for the ski lift. Even the sight of a lift chair was making her queasy.

"Taylor, you're a physics genius," Gabriella reminded her friend. "Just keep thinking about the upward force of the lift, which has been carefully calibrated to overcome the downward force of gravity, and you'll be fine!"

"I know, I know," Taylor moaned. "But even

though my brain knows how the lift works, my stomach is a nervous wreck!"

Troy and Chad were standing a few feet behind the girls, engrossed in their own whispered conversation.

"I know I said this was a good idea last night," Chad hissed. "But that was yesterday! Now that I'm here–" He glanced up at the slope where snowboarders were already doing their runs. One person from a group of tiny, distant figures shot off a snowbank, did a flip in the air, and landed perfectly. Chad shook his head at the sight. "I'm going to look pathetic next to those guys."

"Believe me, everybody's too busy thinking about what they're doing to worry about you," Troy said. "You'll do fine. Besides, you told me you'd tried snowboarding only once before."

Chad eyed him suspiciously. "Yeah? So?"

"So you can't assume that you're lousy after just one try," Troy pointed out. "You might be a great snowboarder and you'll never know it! Are you willing to go through the rest of your life thinking that you're bad at something when maybe you could be great? Are you willing to give up at the very beginning? Are you willing to go home knowing you didn't even try—"

"Okay, okay, *okay.*" Chad laughed. "Enough with the pep talk! I'd rather fall down the mountain at fifty miles an hour than listen to Troy Bolton, Master Motivator!"

"That's what I figured," Troy said with a smile. "Now, here's the first step." He nodded towards Taylor. "Get on the lift chair with Taylor."

Chad gave him a puzzled look. "Be glad to, but . . . why?"

"Because she told Gabriella she's afraid to go on the lift," Troy explained. "We figured that if she sat with you, you could joke around and distract her a little bit."

Chad grinned. "I think I'm up to that challenge."

"Good." Troy gave him a little push. "So get started."

* * *

Troy and Gabriella watched as their friends inched forward in the lift line. Taylor definitely looked nervous. As a chair in front of them lifted a pair of eager skiers off the ground, they saw her clamp one hand over her eyes and clutch Chad's arm with the other. Even standing out of earshot, they could tell that Chad was talking to her a mile a minute.

"If anyone can make Taylor forget that she's dangling hundreds of feet above the ground, it's Chad," Troy said earnestly, pleased with the plan that he and Gabriella had come up with earlier that morning. Troy turned to look at Gabriella and noticed that she suddenly looked nervous.

"Yeah," Gabriella said slowly. " 'Dangling hundreds of feet above the ground.' I guess I never thought of it that way until you mentioned it–"

"Oh, look, there's Ryan standing in the other line," Troy said quickly.

53

"Are you, by any chance, trying to distract me, Troy?" Gabriella grinned.

He smiled at her. "Is it working?"

"Yes, thank you," she said, laughing. She glanced over to where Ryan was standing in the lift line, chatting animatedly to Savannah. Gabriella raised her eyebrows in surprise. She knew Ryan liked Savannah – he kept dropping her name into the conversation, and last night at dinner he kept looking around the room as if he was trying to spot her. But Gabriella was still surprised to see him there, instead of back at the lodge with Sharpay.

"Looks like Ryan really *has* decided to skip practice," she commented.

Suddenly, Ryan glanced up. When he saw Gabriella and Troy watching him, he looked alarmed. He excused himself from Savannah and scurried over to their side.

"Hi, guys," he said worriedly. "Listen, do me a favour, okay? Please don't tell Sharpay that you saw me here this morning. She'll be furious if she knows I ditched rehearsal!" He gave them a serious look. "And you know how scary she is when she's angry."

Troy nodded sympathetically, but Gabriella felt she had to mention one small flaw in Ryan's reasoning. "I think she'll notice that you're not there," she pointed out. "Especially since the rehearsal only involves the two of you."

"I thought of that already," Ryan said with a smile. "I'm going to tell her that I completely forgot about rehearsal. It just slipped my mind!"

Gabriella looked doubtful. "Do you think she'll buy that?"

"Well, it's not *likely*," Ryan admitted, "but, on the other hand, she can't prove that I *didn't* forget, can she? So all I have to do is dodge her until lunchtime, and I'm golden. I'll see you guys later!" he exclaimed, heading back towards Savannah.

"I can't do this, I can't do this, I can't DO this!" Taylor's eyes were wide and fearful as she and

Chad inched forward on the ski-lift line.

Every moment that passed brought her closer to the front of the line and to the moment when she would have to take a seat for that scary trip up the mountain. She turned around and glared at Gabriella. "I can't believe you talked me into this!" she cried.

"Hey, Taylor, calm down!" Chad said reassuringly. He leaned down to scoop up a handful of snow and added jokingly, "I can help you chill out, if you'd like—"

She shot him a menacing look. "Don't you dare!"

He started packing the snow into a ball. "Or else what?" he challenged.

She knelt down and scooped up her own handful of snow. "Or else you'll be going *down*!" she warned him.

He pretended to back away in fear. Taylor tried to remain serious, but she couldn't help it. She burst out laughing.

At that moment, they approached the front of

the line. Before she could think about what she was doing, Chad nudged her into her seat, sat down beside her, and their chair lifted off the ground. Taylor stared nervously ahead.

Just then, the next chair came along and it was time for Gabriella and Troy to get on. She usually wasn't afraid of heights, but she gasped when their chair rose off the ground with a sudden jerk. As it began moving slowly through the air, she stared straight ahead and forced herself to take deep breaths.

Then she felt Troy put his arm around her shoulders. "Relax," he said softly. "You rode the ski lift yesterday, remember? And you're still here."

Instantly, she felt calmer. She turned her head to smile at him. "Thanks. I guess I must have caught a little of Taylor's nerves."

"She looks okay now, though, don't you think?" he said, pointing to the chair in front of them.

Gabriella followed his gaze. Chad and Taylor

were joking and laughing.

"Yeah," she grinned. "Looks like our plan is working!"

As they approached the top of the mountain, they watched as it was Chad and Taylor's turn to jump off the ski lift. Taylor struggled a bit at first, but quickly caught her balance and exited the lift safely. A few moments later, it was Troy and Gabriella's turn to get off. When they joined their friends, Gabriella smiled at a very relieved Taylor.

"See?" she said. "That wasn't so bad, was it?"

"No," Taylor admitted. "But only because Chad didn't stop talking the whole time, making it completely impossible for me to focus on the very important fact that I was dangling hundreds of feet in the air."

Chad bowed. "I live to serve," he said solemnly.

Once they were standing at the top of the trail, though, it was Chad's turn to be worried.

He and Troy stood at the top of the run, a

little distance away from the girls. Chad stared down the mountainside, which now seemed steeper than it had looked from the bottom of the mountain. Much, much steeper.

"I don't know, man," he said uneasily. "Isn't there another way to get to the bottom?"

Troy laughed. "Nope, this is it. Come on, you're a natural athlete! You'll get this in no time."

"I'm a natural athlete on the basketball court," Chad pointed out. "Which is flat. And not icy."

"Here, let's start with a heelside slide," Troy said. "That way, you'll know how to stop. Then we'll move on to a falling leaf pattern and . . . well, that'll probably be it for today. You ready?"

Reluctantly, Chad nodded. "As ready as I'll ever be."

Half an hour later, he decided it was time to revise that statement.

"Why am I doing this again?" he asked Troy

from where he had fallen into a snowbank.

"Because it's fun," Troy said, as he held out his hand to help Chad stand up.

"Oh, fun. Right." A trickle of ice slid down Chad's neck. He shivered. "Thanks for reminding me."

"Well, it's more fun when you get the hang of it," Troy said. "The first couple of days are always the toughest."

"No kidding," Chad said gloomily. "I've spent more time on the ground than on my feet." He kicked at the snow in frustration. "It's this stupid snow! It's like kryptonite to me!"

Gabriella and Taylor edged their way over from where they had just fallen down, just in time to hear this last comment.

"Which would make you Superman, I guess," Taylor commented with a smile.

Chad couldn't help but laugh at that. "More like Clark Kent," he said ruefully, brushing snow off his trousers.

"Tell me about it," Gabriella agreed. Her eyes

were sparkling and her cheeks were pink from the cold. "This is a lot harder than it looks!"

"It's harder to the tenth power," Taylor agreed, laughing. "But what's life without a challenge, right?"

"Right," Gabriella said firmly. "So . . . one more try?"

Taylor nodded and they pushed off the mountain again, laughing hysterically as they careened down the trail. Chad watched them go, then turned to see Troy looking at him thoughtfully.

"Are you going to let Taylor and Gabriella get ahead of us?" Troy teased.

"No way," Chad said quickly. Troy grinned proudly.

"Okay, okay, you are a master motivator, I admit it!" Chad laughed. "Now, come on, show me the way you push off again before they beat us to the bottom of the mountain!"

CHAPTER FIVE

"**R**yan! Where have you been?" Sharpay stormed into the lounge and stood in front of the fireplace, her hands on her hips, and stared at her brother. She was silhouetted against the light from the crackling fire, which made her look even more intimidating to Ryan than usual. "You missed rehearsal!"

He gazed up at her, trying to look innocent. Unfortunately, that meant that he opened his eyes very wide and didn't blink, which got to be fairly uncomfortable.

"I waited in the club for an hour!" Sharpay continued. "Why didn't you show up?"

"Oh, we were supposed to rehearse again today? I'm sorry, I thought it was tomorrow. . . ." Even as he said it, Ryan realized how lame his excuse sounded, but he was never that quick with a comeback.

"*Ri*-ight." Sharpay didn't look even a little bit convinced. "I don't suppose that girl had anything to do with your shocking lack of professionalism?"

His plan hadn't worked too well so far, and Ryan was out of ideas. He looked at Sharpay innocently. "What girl?"

She smirked. "Oh, you know, the one named after a city in Georgia," she said, rolling her eyes. "Atlanta?"

Ryan glared at his sister. "If you mean *Savannah*," he said stiffly, "it just so happens that I did spend the morning with her–"

"What?!" Sharpay shrieked.

"–because I am on *holiday*, Sharpay!" he said loudly. "We all are! It's great that you want to enter the contest, but why not just jump on the stage and sing on the spur of the moment, like everybody else?"

She gasped. "I can't believe I'm hearing this," she said, shaking her head. "Perform without *practising*? Have you lost your mind?"

Before Ryan could answer, Kelsi walked in, holding a sheaf of music paper. Her face lit up when she saw them.

"Hi, guys," she called out. "Guess what. I just wrote a new song–"

"Wonderful," Sharpay snapped. "Ryan, you need to make a choice right now–"

Kelsi plopped down on the sofa. "I think it's actually pretty good," she said quietly. "But I really need to hear someone sing it, so I was wondering–"

Sharpay continued to ignore her. All her attention was focused on her brother, who was getting that stubborn look that she had started seeing more and more these days. Ever since he had started hanging out with the Wildcats over the summer, in fact. "Do you want to enter the contest with me or not?" she asked in annoyance.

"If it means spending all my free time rehearsing," Ryan replied angrily, "then no, I don't!"

"Fine!" Sharpay yelled. "Then you're fired!"

"You can't fire me!" he yelled back. "I quit!"

Kelsi was looking wide-eyed from Sharpay to Ryan. She expected some sort of explosive reaction from Sharpay, but apparently Sharpay couldn't think of a suitably scathing response.

"What-*ever*," Sharpay said finally, turning on her heel. She strode out of the room.

Kelsi and Ryan both sighed with relief at the same time, then they caught each other's eye and giggled.

"Sorry," Ryan said. He wondered briefly how many times he had apologized for Sharpay over the years, then decided that it wasn't worth trying to count. "She's a little on edge because of this karaoke contest."

"I kind of guessed as much," Kelsi said, smiling.

Ryan glanced down at the composition papers she was holding. "What were you saying about writing a new song?"

Her face lit up. "Oh, yes! I was just playing around on the piano after breakfast and, all of a sudden, this music just started coming to me. I usually have to work on a song for a couple of weeks, but this one . . . it seemed to appear out of nowhere."

"Wow. That's pretty cool." Ryan was impressed.

"Well, yeah." Kelsi's smile faded a bit. "Of course, maybe that means it's not any good. That's why I wanted to hear someone sing it . . ."

"Let me see." Ryan took the papers from her and began reading the music. "Hey, this looks great!" He glanced up. "You know, this gives me an idea. . . ."

"Hello?" Sharpay said into the microphone. "Testing, one, two, three." She winced at the blast of feedback that screeched through the empty club room.

"Sorry, sorry!" Sammy cried, popping up from behind the bank of electronic equipment. He was actually a high school student who had a part-time job at the resort because, as he had explained to Sharpay, his uncle worked in the accounting department. "Plus, I'm a pro when it comes to audio stuff," he had boasted. "I'm pretty much a genius, actually."

He didn't sound like much of a genius, Sharpay thought with irritation. He couldn't even get the microphone to work properly! And he didn't look like one, either. His round face was sweating as he nervously twiddled with various wires.

"Hold on," he said. "I'll get this fixed in just one minute. . . ."

Sharpay tapped her fingers impatiently on the

microphone. She wasn't used to waiting. She didn't like waiting. And she was certainly not in the mood to do something she disliked.

Screech!

Her head snapped around and she scowled at Sammy, who was now crawling behind the audio equipment. He couldn't see her angry look, but he must have felt it, because one hand waved apologetically above the speakers. "Almost there!" he shouted.

"We'd better be!" she yelled back. "I don't have all day, you know!"

Sharpay started pacing back and forth, trying to calm down. Actually, that was the problem, she thought. She *did* have all day to waste. She had no one to hang out with. After his fight with Sharpay, Ryan had headed to the ski slopes with Savannah. And after making such a point about how she had to rehearse, she would feel silly if she backed down and asked the others if she could join them.

She stopped at the edge of the stage and

looked down. She was wearing one of her favourite costumes, a pink-and-purple ruffled dress, with strappy high-heeled pink shoes. Usually, just putting this costume on lifted her mood. Today, however . . .

"Sammy!" she yelled.

"I got it!" He stood up, beaming. "Try the mic now."

She took a deep breath. If it still wasn't working, she was really going to be furious! But as she turned it on, the feedback was gone. Her voice echoed around the room. Sharpay smiled. She couldn't help it; she just loved hearing her own voice.

"Well, finally," she said with a huff. "Okay, start my music. . . ."

She struck a pose, and as the music blared out, she began to dance across the stage. For the next few minutes, she gave her performance everything she had, just as she planned to do on New Year's Eve. She finished with a high kick and a twirl, and ended in another triumphant pose, her hands held high above her head.

The music stopped. Sharpay stood in place, smiling brightly. There was nothing that she loved more than performing.

Suddenly, she spotted Sammy staring at her in awe. He was clapping and standing on his feet. "Bravo!" he yelled.

"Actually, it's *brava*," Sharpay corrected him, "since I'm a girl." But she smiled with satisfaction and walked down the steps towards where Sammy was standing.

"You were awesome!" he exclaimed.

"Naturally." She tossed her hair and gave him a knowing smile.

"You're going to win the contest for sure," he went on earnestly. "No one else will even come close!"

"Hmm." Sharpay stopped smiling. She had heard those words before. In fact, she had even said those words to Ryan, when Troy and Gabriella first signed up for the *Twinkle Towne* auditions. She had been sure she would

THROW YOUR OWN FABULOUS EAST HIGH PARTY!

If I'm going to a party, I want it to be the most fabulous party possible. I've asked all of our East High friends to share their top tips with you for how to have a wonderful winter celebration. If there's one thing I know about, it's how to be fabulous. So read on and you just might learn something!

Sharpay

DECORATE LIKE YOU MEAN IT

SNOWY SCENE

Whether or not you live somewhere snowy, you're going to need a wintery look indoors to have an authentic winter party – buy some fake snow in a can and spray it on sprigs of holly and other green plants. You could even decorate the mirrors and windows with a snowy scene!

GLORIOUS GLITTER

If you think balloons are for kids then you should think again. Use a funnel or tube to pour some glitter into a balloon before you blow it up. That way, when they get popped, they'll blow a beautiful spray of glitter into the air that'll make the whole room come alive!

HAPPY HEADGEAR

The time-honoured tradition of the party hat is one that is not to be sneered at lightly. Hats are fun and fabulous – just look at me! Of course, you can't always expect your guests to bring their own, so keep a box of glamorous, glitzy hats to make sure everyone will be dressed up to add to the party vibe!

LOVELY LIGHTS

Nothing screams "bad party" like an over-lit location. My personal favourite is to set the scene with some fairy lights. Turn off the main light and switch to mood lighting with some well-placed fairy lights – they're sure to melt the hardest of hearts, maybe even in your direction!

THE RIGHT INVITE

You want to make sure your party invitation speaks from the heart – this is Gabriella's guide to making a truly beautiful invitation card.

1. Firstly, you'll need some thick paper.

2. Use a pencil to faintly write out your invitation text. Once you're happy with it, go over the words in ink. See the example below for what you should include.
(Don't forget to rub out the lines once the ink is dry!)

You want your guests to feel special, so carefully write their names here.

Dear ....
You are invited to a fabulous party
....
....
R.S.V.P to ....

Make sure you tell them exactly when and where it will be!

Give people a phone number or email address so that they can R.S.V.P. That way you know exactly who's coming to the party.

3. Once the ink is all dry and your invitation text is ready, find some gold and silver glitter, and a glue stick with a thin tip.

4. Draw some pretty shapes, like stars, on the outer edges of the card with the glue stick. Sprinkle gold and silver glitter over the card and then shake off the excess glitter. Leave the invitiations to dry and then watch them sparkle!

MAGICAL MUSIC

Party karaoke isn't necessarily for everyone, but even those who don't want to be show-stopping solo stars will appreciate a good sing-along. Here are a few of my East High favourites for perfect party moments!

START OF SOMETHING NEW

Troy and Gabriella found their stride with this song at the New Year's Eve party. This song is really uplifting. Who will you sing it with?

BOP TO THE TOP

This is a lively tune that's bound to get the whole room tapping their feet! Personally, I'd recommend some fabulous choreographed dance moves to go with it, but everyone has to find their own style!

WE'RE ALL IN THIS TOGETHER

This will get everyone singing and dancing. But be sure to build up to it as it's a real show-stopper!

THE BEST OF THE GUESTS

I have some clear ideas on what makes an A-list guest list for the perfect party. Follow these tips for total success.

1. Deciding on the first people to invite is really easy. It'd be so weird to throw a party without having any of my family there to enjoy it too, so I'd be sure to invite them. Which members of your family would you invite?

2. I can't imagine spending a special party night without my best friends. Make sure you write out a list of your closest buddies to invite – you don't want to miss off anyone obvious!

3. The more people that come to your party, the better, so everyone can have fun together. Once you've made a list of your nearest and dearest, don't forget to think about the other people you might have missed off, like neighbours, teachers, and other kids in school. This could be your chance to make more close friends, so get into the party spirit!

ENJOY YOUR FABULOUS EAST HIGH STYLE PARTY

win – but what had happened? Her first professional setback!

She frowned at the memory of how devastated she was losing out to Gabriella. Fortunately, her thoughts were interrupted by Sammy, who was continuing to compliment her in a most satisfactory way.

"I mean, I've heard a lot of people sing karaoke here," he continued. "Too many people, to tell you the truth. None of them could hold a candle to you."

She tilted her head to one side and gave him an appraising glance. "That's very sweet of you," she said. "But sometimes judges can be rather, well, irrational. If only there was some way to make sure that I was going to win . . ."

Sammy just stared at her, his round face puzzled. "Believe me, you won't have any competition–"

"Perhaps not," she said crisply. "But I happen to know that two people in particular are going to enter the contest, and those two people have a history of winning auditions that they have no business winning. I would like . . ." She paused to give him a long, meaningful look. ". . . to make sure that doesn't happen on New Year's Eve."

Sammy gulped. He had a feeling she was going to ask him to do something that, strictly speaking, an ethical audio engineer should not do. And Sammy took the audio engineer's code of honour very seriously.

"I really want to win this contest," she said, feigning innocence. "It would mean so much to me if you could help me–"

Sammy couldn't resist Sharpay's charm and let out a sigh. "What do you have in mind?" he asked slowly.

Sharpay smiled contentedly and leaned forward to whisper in his ear.

Sharpay was humming as she left Sammy in the club adjusting the sound hookup. Now that her work was done for the day, she felt like getting some fresh air. She'd just run upstairs, change into her ski clothes, and head for the mountain. She couldn't wait to hit the slopes.

As she crossed the entrance hall, she spotted Matt, the cute ski-rescue guy, talking to a girl whose right ankle was bandaged with a temporary splint.

Sharpay's gaze sharpened with displeasure as she saw who else was standing next to them: Ryan and that girl he insisted on hanging out with. What was her name? Sharpay searched her memory. Oh, yes. *Savannah.*

Sharpay's lip curled as she watched the other girl, who was apparently Savannah's friend, gaze adoringly up at Matt. "Honestly, I can't thank you enough!" the girl gushed, flicking a jet-black curl over her shoulder. "I don't know what I would have done if you hadn't found me!"

"It was no big deal." Matt shrugged, but he looked pleased. "Just doing my job."

"I know it's your job, but that doesn't make it

any less heroic!" Savannah exclaimed. "Jeanine twisted her ankle so badly, she couldn't take one step. She could have frozen to death!"

"Well, that's why I'm here, to help in just that kind of situation." Whatever he had done, Matt was clearly trying to play it down. Even from where Sharpay stood, she could see him blush a little.

"At least let me buy you a hot chocolate to show my appreciation," Jeanine went on. "It's the least I can do."

Matt gave her a friendly grin. "Sure," he said. "Why not?"

Sharpay watched through narrowed eyes as they walked towards the dining hall. As hard as she had tried, she hadn't been able to get Matt to hold a five-minute conversation with her, let alone sit down for a cosy cup of hot chocolate! Clearly, something was seriously wrong with the universe. . . .

At that moment, Ryan spotted her and then pretended he didn't see her. He whispered something to Savannah and began trying to edge his way out of the room.

"Ryan!" Sharpay called. She raced over to where her brother and Savannah stood.

"Oh, hi, Sharpay." He smiled nervously. "Where have you been? I haven't seen you in ages."

"Of course, you haven't," she snapped. "Because *I* have been in rehearsal, which has been going fantastically well."

"That's wonderful," Savannah said diplomatically. "Ryan has told me what a great singer you are. We're all looking forward to hearing you at the contest."

Sharpay hesitated, momentarily thrown off-balance by the compliment. She quickly recovered, however. "Of course you are," she said with a toss of her head. Then she added, in a deliberately casual voice, "So, what happened to your friend's ankle?"

Savannah's eyes widened. "Oh, it was so scary! She was skiing yesterday and got a little off course and went into a gully!"

"Which wouldn't have been a problem," Ryan chimed in, "except that she hurt her ankle and couldn't climb out."

"We saw it happen, so I stayed with Jeanine while Ryan went to tell the ski rescue team." She beamed proudly at Ryan. "I don't know what I would have done if Ryan hadn't been there!"

Now it was Ryan's turn to blush. "I'm just glad I could get help," he said shyly. "And that Jeanine was all right. You know, accidents like that can be pretty scary. . . ."

He kept talking, but Sharpay soon tuned him out. She was too busy thinking about what she had just learned. First, and most importantly, she had learned that if someone got in trouble skiing, Matt would rescue them. But she had also realized that the rescued person would probably get a lot of attention, especially from Matt. And if that happened, Sharpay reasoned, other people (like, say, Troy) would probably become quite jealous. All of which could lead to a delightful situation in which Sharpay had not one, but two cute guys vying for her attention!

All of which gave Sharpay her second brilliant idea of the day.

CHAPTER SIX

Back on the mountain, Chad balanced carefully on his snowboard. He pushed off and zoomed down the slope. "Okay," he yelled. "Here I go . . ." He hit a bump, lofted into the air . . . and landed perfectly!

"Awesome!" Troy yelled.

Gabriella and Taylor cheered and clapped. Jason and Zeke, who had joined them, added whoops of enthusiasm to the general commotion.

Grinning, Chad took a bow, then climbed back up to where the others were still standing.

"Man, that felt awesome!" he exclaimed. "You were right, Troy. It was worth all those face-plants in the snow, just to be able to do an aerial once in my life."

"I told you that you could do it," Troy said, laughing.

"You looked great," Taylor said with unusual warmth. When he looked at her suspiciously, she nodded. "Really. I'm not kidding."

He broke out in a grin. "Thanks. So, I noticed that you were having a few problems with your wheelie. Feel like taking a lesson from an awesome snowboarder such as myself?"

Taylor rolled her eyes, laughing. "Sure," she replied. "Just take it slow, hotshot."

As Chad and Taylor moved away to work on their wheelies, Jason and Zeke hopped on their snowboards and went careening down the hill. Troy and Gabriella watched, wincing a bit as Jason wiped out and slid on his back for several feet. Zeke followed suit a few seconds later, sliding right into Jason.

"Do you think they need help?" Gabriella asked. She sounded concerned.

Troy squinted to see better, then shook his head, grinning. "I can hear them laughing from here," he said. "I think they're fine."

"Oh, good," she said, relieved. For a moment, no other skiers or snowboarders were around; there was silence except for the wind in the trees. Gabriella looked over at Troy and smiled. "You know, I love being here with all of our friends, but this is kind of nice, too. Just the two of us," she said shyly.

Immediately, she looked down. What if Troy would rather be around a group of people, instead of alone with her? What if all he cared about was hanging out with his buddies? Gabriella felt so embarrassed. What if she had just made a complete and total fool of herself?

As she struggled to come up with something

else to say, Troy smiled. "I know," he said. "Like last year, right?"

"Right!" A wave of relief rushed through Gabriella. "That was really special for me, Troy."

"Me, too," he agreed. "I guess I kind of thought it would happen again, but I didn't really think through how different this trip would be. With Chad and Taylor and everybody here, too."

Suddenly, their attention was diverted by a loud yell. They turned to see that Chad and Taylor had tried another run and had both fallen down near Jason and Zeke, who were taking advantage of the moment to pelt them with snowballs. Troy laughed and shook his head. "As much fun as those guys are, it's not the same as just hanging out with you."

Gabriella felt her heart beat a little faster. "I'm so glad you feel the same way." She smiled.

"Of course I do!" He smiled back at her. "Let's make sure we find some time to sit by the fire tonight, okay? And we can have hot chocolate together in that little stand by the ice-skating rink tomorrow? And then on New Year's—"

"We'll sing karaoke!" Gabriella interrupted, laughing. "Sounds perfect!"

"Great," he said. "But first, we have to get to the bottom of this mountain."

"Oh. Right." Gabriella peered down the icy slope, with a hesitant look on her face. "I'm not sure I've got the hang of this, though. . . ."

"You did great yesterday," Troy said encouragingly. "Before you know it, you'll be doing aerials."

Gabriella giggled.

He looked at her. "What?"

"It's just that you're such a coach!" she exclaimed. "I mean, so far I've only managed to go two feet without falling over, but you still act like I'm doing a fantastic job."

He crossed his arms and pretended to give her a stern look. "Are you still out here on the mountain, trying your hardest?" he asked.

"Well, yes," Gabriella admitted.

He grinned. "Then I stand by what I said.

You're doing great." He motioned for her to get on her snowboard. "I noticed yesterday that you seem to be leaning forward a little too much. Let me show you something that might help—"

Suddenly, Troy was interrupted by a skier zooming down the mountain in a pink blur, then stopping a few feet away with a showy turn of her skis that sent a spray of snow into Gabriella's face.

"Oops, I'm so sorry!" Sharpay called out cheerily.

"No problem," Gabriella said, as she wiped the snow off her cheeks. "I'll just think of this as a free facial!"

Troy laughed, and Sharpay rolled her eyes. "You *do* know that facials are warm, right?" she commented. Gabriella sighed. Sharpay always had a response for everything!

"So, what's up, Sharpay?" Troy asked. "I thought you were too busy with rehearsals to hit the slopes."

"Well, it would be a waste to spend my whole holiday inside. Besides," she added loftily, "Ryan and I have made many good friends on the ski circuit. After all, skiers go to all the ritziest places: Tahoe, St. Moritz, Aspen. It was such fun to see some of our old pals, check out the latest fashions in ski-wear, find out who's going to be in the Caribbean next month, that sort of thing."

Gabriella kept smiling and barely managed not to roll her eyes.

"Of course, skiers usually don't mix with *snowboarders*," Sharpay continued. "But I saw you guys down here so I just thought I'd say hi."

"That's so nice of you, Sharpay," Troy said seriously. "We really appreciate you going out of your way to say hello. Especially since we're not dressed in the latest snowboarding fashion."

She looked at what Troy and Gabriella were wearing – old ski pants, shabby jackets, and mismatched gloves – and raised an eyebrow. "Clearly. Although to be fair, I don't think there is such a thing as snowboarding fashion, *is* there?"

Troy looked down at himself and remembered that last year he had patched his sleeve with duct tape, which was now shredding and grey. "Now that you mention it," he said, "no, there's not."

Sharpay gave him a warm smile. "Don't worry about it, Troy," she said. "You always look great, no matter what you're wearing."

Oh, brother, Gabriella thought. Sharpay really knows how to work it when she wants to. She is relentless!

"Well, I think I'll continue on my run," Sharpay said. "I'm going to head that way." She pointed to a trail that led off to a little-used part of the mountain.

Gabriella frowned. "Are you sure you'll be all right by yourself? It doesn't look like many people use that trail."

"Exactly!" Sharpay looked extremely pleased at this comment. Then she seemed to catch herself and add, "I mean, that's why I want to try it. Sometimes having all these people around is just too much when one has a sensitive and artistic soul like mine. Sometimes one just wants to get away from the crowds and connect, alone, with nature! Sometimes one must find solitude to refresh the spirit in order to face a new day!"

"Right," Troy said. "And sometimes one makes a big mistake by going off on her own at the end of the day."

"Honestly, Troy, you're acting as if I haven't been skiing practically my whole life!" She tossed her head. "I'll be fine. After all, I'm just going" – she pointed again with dramatic emphasis – "over there." She swept off with a whoosh of her skis.

As they watched her go, Gabriella gave Troy a troubled look. "Are you sure she'll be okay? It *is* getting dark . . ."

"Oh, you know Sharpay," he said casually. "She just has to make every move she makes sound dramatic. When she gets to her solitary spot in nature and realizes there's not an audience there, she'll get back to the lodge as fast as she can."

"You're right about that," Gabriella laughed.

"Now, how about that trick I was going to show you?" Troy said.

Sharpay skied down the trail, feeling smug. Just as she had planned, Troy and Gabriella knew where she was going. They both looked a little worried. And they were sure to notice if she didn't turn up for dinner.

As she got to the last turn, she slowed, then deliberately turned to ski off into a small stand of trees. This was the way she would go if she had lost control and been unable to make it to the end of the run. This was the natural place that any-one – and anyone, of course, meant Matt, her potential rescuer – would search as soon as her friends realized that she was missing. This was, in other words, the perfect place to stage her rescue.

After she had skied several dozen feet into the

woods, she stopped and looked around. The light from the setting sun gilded the snow a rosy gold; the sky overhead was rapidly darkening to a deep, intense blue. A few stars appeared, twinkling in the fast-approaching night sky.

Sharpay sighed deeply with satisfaction. As usual, she had come up with the perfect plan. Everything was going just as she had hoped. Now all she had to do was settle down and wait.

CHAPTER SEVEN

"**B**rrr!" Chad rubbed his hands together as he entered the lodge. "The snow today was totally awesome, but I'm glad to get inside where it's warm!"

Taylor nodded. "The temperature really drops when the sun goes down." Her eyes brightened as she saw the fire roaring in the fireplace. "I say let's take our boots off and warm up by the fire. Maybe play a board game?"

"Sounds like an excellent idea," Troy replied.

"Although it does bring up another question . . ."

Gabriella knew what was coming, but she laughed and said what she knew Troy wanted her to say anyway. "What question is that, Troy?"

"Is anyone brave enough to take on" – he raised his arms in a victory pose – "the reigning Scrabble champion?"

A chorus of good-natured boos greeted this challenge. They had played six Scrabble games in a row the night before. Troy had won them all, thanks to his previously unknown talent for using the letter "X".

"Not if I have to look up the word 'xenon' again," Jason said. "Or 'lexicon'. Reading the dictionary reminds me too much of sixth-period English."

"Ooh, how about a little snack?" Zeke interrupted. His eyes had caught sight of a dessert buffet set up along one wall. "Those snickerdoodles look delicious. And they would be very tasty with some hot chocolate–"

"I don't know about that," said Mrs Montez,

who had just entered the room with Troy's mum and overheard Zeke's suggestion. "We're having dinner in an hour. You don't want to spoil your appetite."

"Believe me, I could eat everything on that buffet and still finish my dinner," Zeke said earnestly. "Snowboarding all afternoon really makes you hungry."

"Judging the way these boys go through my refrigerator after practice, I'm sure that's true," Mrs Bolton commented to Mrs Montez.

"Is that a 'yes, we can have a few cookies'?" Troy asked. "Since dinner is a very long sixty minutes away?"

"Oh, why not, it's a holiday!" Mrs Montez exclaimed, smiling. "In fact, I think I might join you!"

Laughing, they all headed for the dessert table, where they were faced with the impossible choice of apple turnovers versus snickerdoodles versus cups of caramel popcorn . . . and ended up getting one of each treat and sharing them all.

* * *

In the forest, night was quickly approaching. Sharpay shivered as she watched the light from the setting sun leave the sky. Away from the lights of the ski run and the lodge building, she was alone in darkness deeper than any she had ever been in before.

The night was also completely silent and still. No sound of rescuers calling her name. No noise from friends crashing through the snow to reach her. No hint, in fact, that anyone was looking for her at all. . . .

They're all back at the lodge now, she thought. They're probably about to eat dinner. That's when they'll notice I'm not there.

She felt a little relieved at that thought, but the moment didn't last.

Her stomach was beginning to growl, and she wished the thought of dinner had not entered her mind.

And the silence of the woods was not as complete as she had first thought. In fact, every once in a while, she heard a rustle in the bushes that sounded sinister. Like a bear or a wolf or some other wild animal that was also feeling rather hungry . . .

Sharpay started stomping the ground, partly to keep her feet warm and partly to scare off any scary creatures in the vicinity.

If I am killed and eaten by a bear, she thought fiercely, everyone is going to be very, very sorry!

Somehow, this thought did not cheer her up at all.

"I swear, 'divaphobia' is actually a real word," Troy laughed.

"Fine," Gabriella said teasingly. "Then what's the definition?"

"It means, um, the fear of being trapped in a small space with someone who has a large ego," he replied in a serious tone.

Chad led the group in booing this bluff. Then he threw a piece of caramel popcorn at Troy for good measure. "Nice try," he quipped.

"But everyone knows the word for that is 'Sharpayphobia'!"

He glanced around the room, hoping that Sharpay was close enough to have overheard his joke. Chad loved teasing Sharpay. She always took the bait, and it was quite fun to see her get mad at him.

Just then, Zeke came in, looking worried. "Hey, I was just looking for Sharpay to see if she wanted any of these desserts, but I can't find her," he said. "Does anyone know where she is?"

"Still rehearsing?" Kelsi guessed.

"Trying on all her costumes one more time?" Taylor suggested.

"Getting ready for her close-up?" Jason offered.

Everyone laughed, except Zeke.

"Seriously, guys, I haven't seen her all night," he said with concern in his voice. "Ryan said she hasn't been around for hours. And I just went to the club, and she's not there, either."

Zeke's words started to sink in as everyone sat in silence for a moment. They looked at each other in alarm.

"We'd better tell my dad," Troy said. "Just in case . . ."

"When was the last time anyone saw Sharpay?" Matt looked around at the Wildcats, a serious expression on his face. Two other members of the ski rescue team stood with him, ready to launch a search.

"She skied over to where Gabriella and I were snowboarding this afternoon," Troy volunteered. "That was about four-thirty, I guess."

Gabriella looked concerned. "She said she was going to try a trail that wasn't used too much," she reported. "We told her it might not be a good idea, but she wouldn't listen. Maybe we should have been more insistent," she added softly.

No one said anything, but everyone had the same thought. When Sharpay wanted to do something, she did it.

Matt exchanged glances with the other members of the team. "Show us where the trail was," he said, spreading out a map. "And what direction she was heading. . . ."

The moon shone brightly in the jet black sky. It was a beautiful night, but Sharpay was in no mood to appreciate it. The strange noises hadn't stopped. And hours seemed to have passed with no sign of help.

That's when she remembered herl phone! She unzipped her pocket, pulled it out, and flipped it open, relief washing through her body . . . until she saw the screen.

NO NETWORK AVAILABLE.

Sharpay glared up at the mountains that blocked thel phone signal. This is so totally unfair, she thought. What's the use of owning the very latest mobile technology when it doesn't work when you need it most!

As she wrapped her arms around herself, her teeth chattering, she had to admit that, for once, her scheming nature had seemingly let her down. In fact, the longer she stood in the dark and the cold, the more she realized that this definitely hadn't been one of her better ideas.

"Sharpay! Can you hear me?"

"Hello? Sharpay? Yell if you can hear us!"

The members of the ski rescue team trudged through the woods, yelling out for Sharpay every few feet, then stopping to wait for an answer.

"Sharpay! Where are you?"

Standing on the terrace, Troy and Gabriella could hear the rescue team's shouts, though they gradually began to fade as they moved farther away.

Troy turned to Gabriella. "I can't believe we let her go off on her own like that," he said quietly.

"I know," she agreed. "At least she told us where she was going." She pointed to the searchers' torches bobbing in the distance. "I'm

97

sure someone will find her soon."

"Yeah," Troy said. "I sure hope so."

"What in the world was I thinking?" Sharpay thought out loud. She could see puffs of breath with each word she spoke, which only reminded her of how cold she was. "How could I have been such an idiot?"

A tear slid down her cheek. She brushed it away before it froze there.

Suddenly, a voice rang out through the frigid air. She looked up, alert.

"Sharpay!" the voice called again. "Where are you?"

"Here!" she screamed, jumping up and down. "Over here!"

Moments later, a figure crashed through the bushes. It was Matt. She threw her arms around him, sobbing with relief. "Oh, thank goodness you found me!" she cried.

"You're not hurt? Good. Let's get you inside where it's warm," he said briskly.

By the time Sharpay had arrived back at the lodge, she was exhausted. But once she spotted the Wildcats crowding anxiously around her, her spirits revived. When she was settled on a sofa in front of the fire, holding a cup of hot chocolate and eating a grilled cheese sandwich, Sharpay was actually enjoying the drama of her experience.

". . . And then, just when I thought all hope was lost, I looked around and saw Matt!" she exclaimed, smiling up at him. "That's when I knew that everything would be fine."

"Uh-huh," he said, not smiling back. "But it could have been a lot worse, you know. You could have been hurt, or we might not have found you that easily. So, in the future, you'll know better than to go skiing off by yourself, right?"

Sharpay frowned slightly. She wasn't used to being scolded, and she *certainly* wasn't used to her flirting being ignored – but then she remembered how lonely and cold and scared she had been. "Right," Sharpay said softly. "I'll be more careful, I promise."

"Good." He spotted a couple of the other members of the ski rescue team waving him over. "Well, have a happy New Year's Eve tomorrow, everybody," he said, pausing to give Sharpay one last warning look. "And a *safe* one."

After he left, everyone decided to have one more cup of hot chocolate before it was time for bed. Zeke hurried over to get two cups and then carefully carried them back to Sharpay.

"I'm really glad you're okay," he said, handing a cup to her. "I was really worried."

"Were you?" She gave him a small smile and took a sip of her drink.

"Yes. I told everyone something was up when I couldn't find you anywhere. Everyone assumed you were trying on costumes for your performance tomorrow or rehearsing with Ryan."

"Really?" Sharpay looked unsettled by this news. "So if you hadn't said something, it might have been hours before they started searching?"

He shrugged. "I guess so."

She put her cup down very carefully. Her hands were shaking. "So I might have been out there in the wilderness *all night*?"

Zeke looked at her carefully. "Don't get upset, Sharpay," he said, trying to calm her down. "After all, you're safe and sound now—"

"Because of you!" Sharpay exclaimed. She stared at him for a long moment and then threw her arms around him. "Thank you, thank you, thank you," she gushed. "I don't know how to thank you!"

Zeke looked surprised, and then very, very happy. "That's okay," he grinned. "That's what friends are for."

"No, I mean it," she said, looking at him with gratitude. "I really don't know how to thank you."

He looked at Sharpay and smiled. "You don't have to thank me, Sharpay. Just don't scare me like that ever again!"

CHAPTER EIGHT

The next evening was New Year's Eve! The teen club was already packed with people wearing shiny paper hats and tooting horns when the Wildcats arrived. The dance floor was crowded and everyone was moving to the high-energy music blaring through the speakers. The gang grinned at each other.

"This is going to be a great party!" Chad shouted.

"It'll be off the hook!" Troy agreed. He

high-fived Chad, then Zeke, then Jason.

"Yeah," Jason said, "as long we don't have to get on the stage and sing." Kelsi gave Jason a nervous smile and nodded.

Just then, the MC bounded out on the stage and grabbed the microphone. "Okay, it's time to get this party started! And what better way to celebrate than with a karaoke contest!"

The room erupted into cheers. "So, who's going to kick things off for us?" the MC continued. He looked around the room. A group of teens were yelling and pointing to two boys in their group.

"Ah, I see some volunteers!" the MC went on. "You two, get on up here!"

The two boys sheepishly approached the stage, after much prodding and joking from their friends. Once their song began blasting over the sound system, however, they started getting into their performance, and even broke out a few rock 'n' roll moves that had the crowd laughing and cheering.

Taylor winced as the boys finished their song with an ear-piercing wail. "Wow, that brings a whole new meaning to the word 'pain,'" she said. She gave Gabriella a sideways glance. "I thought you said that karaoke was an *enjoyable* activity?"

"It is," Gabriella laughed, "as long as you don't take it *too* seriously."

"Those two guys sure didn't," Taylor sniffed as the two boys left the stage to a round of applause from their friends.

"Er, yes, thank you, Aaron and Chris, for that . . . um, *spirited* version of 'Can't Wait to Get You Back,'" the MC said, ushering the singers off the stage with relief. He looked around the room and spotted the Wildcats. "All right, how about some new singers?" He looked in Chad's direction.

"Oh, great," Chad muttered, trying to duck out of sight. "I hate it when this happens!"

"Don't be shy! Pick a song and get on up here!" the MC said.

Taylor gave Chad a sly smile. "Come on, Chad,

you can't be any worse than those two."

"You might be surprised," he muttered. "Anyway, getting on stage isn't my thing."

Troy grinned. He couldn't believe his normally self-confident friend was acting so shy. "Hey, dude, I know you can sing," Troy said. "At least, I think that's what you're doing in the locker room while you're getting dressed."

Chad shook his head vigorously. "Me? Sing? No, no, no, you must be mistaken, you've *never* heard me sing—"

"That's true," Zeke said, straight-faced. "The sounds you make are more like a coyote howling at the moon."

"A coyote who howls off-key," Jason added, smiling.

Zeke laughed and gave Jason a high five.

"Right!" Chad exclaimed, looking harassed. "Which is exactly why I don't want to—"

"Get up here on the stage!" The MC's voice boomed out over the PA system as the club spotlight swung around and landed on Chad.

The crowd applauded. "Let's see what kind of chops you have!" the MC exclaimed.

Taylor snickered. "Looks like you don't have a choice, Chad."

"Oh, yeah?" Chad got a determined look on his face. "Well, then, you don't have a choice either!" He grabbed her hand and began walking through the crowd.

"What?" Taylor's expression changed from gleeful to absolutely terrified. "Oh, no—"

"Oh, yes," he said, grinning, as he pulled her up on stage.

"Woo-hoo!" The Wildcats laughed and applauded as Chad and Taylor finished their song with a goofy bow.

At first, Taylor had looked as if she were trying to decide whether to faint or to start yelling at Chad for getting her into this situation. Then the music started. Chad grabbed the mic and started singing a ludicrously over-the-top version of an old sixties song. As usual, Taylor couldn't stay mad at him for long. Before she knew it, he had handed her the mic and she had started in on the second verse — and the crowd had begun cheering her on. By the end, she and Chad were sharing the microphone and singing their hearts out.

As she ran off the stage, she was grinning from ear to ear.

"You don't look like you enjoyed that at all, Taylor," Gabriella said teasingly.

"All right, point taken," Taylor said, laughing and trying to catch her breath. "It was more fun than I expected, I have to admit."

"Oh, look!" Gabriella grabbed Taylor's arm and pointed at the stage. "I can't believe it!"

Taylor followed her gaze and began laughing even harder. Jason and Zeke had decided to sing together. They had chosen an old country song and were belting it out with an exaggerated twang that had the whole room cracking up. They finished to wild applause.

Now that the ice had been broken, the rest of

the Wildcats couldn't wait to get on stage. The worse they sounded, the more fun everyone had. Gabriella sang with Jason, then Taylor sang with Zeke. Troy did a solo Elvis Presley impersonation that had the audience singing along. Even Kelsi got up the courage to perform when she, Gabriella, and Taylor sang backup for Chad, who was doing a Motown number.

"This is fun, isn't it? To get everybody singing with someone different?" Troy asked Gabriella.

She nodded. "It's just like what happened last year at school," she said. "When the jocks finally started talking to the drama students—"

"—and the brainiacs finally started talking to the jocks," he laughed. "You're right. Karaoke seems to have a magical power to get people together — even people who thought they had nothing in common!"

Gabriella glanced over Troy's shoulder, and her smile suddenly slipped away. "Hmm," she said. "There's one person who doesn't seem to be having a very good time."

Troy turned to see Sharpay sitting in the back, watching the performances with a puzzled expression. Everyone was having so much fun, Sharpay thought to herself. She couldn't understand it. Didn't they realize how terrible they sounded? How could they laugh and joke around when they were embarrassing themselves in front of an audience?

She watched as Ryan took the stage and held out his hand to help Savannah up the stairs. He was going to sing with . . . Savannah? She couldn't believe it, but, sure enough, they launched into a chorus of a popular pop song. Of course, Sharpay thought, Ryan didn't sound nearly as good without her but, oddly, he didn't seem to care.

Well, she'd just let everyone do their best, then she'd step on stage and steal the show, Sharpay thought confidently. In fact, it was probably about time to make her move . . . .

She jumped up from her seat to signal to the MC that she wanted her turn at the mic. But before she could get his attention, her view was blocked by Zeke, who stepped right in front of her.

"Excuse me!" she snapped. "I am about to go on stage!"

"I know," he said. "And I would love to go on stage to sing with you!"

Her mouth dropped open. "Are you crazy? I've been rehearsing my act for days – a solo act, I might add! And you, you . . . have you ever even sung a note before tonight?"

"Nope," he admitted cheerfully. "But remember last night? When you said you didn't know how to thank me for noticing that you were missing and getting the ski rescue guys to search for you? I changed my mind and thought this would be a perfect way to thank me!"

Sharpay blushed at how quickly she had forgotten the relief and gratitude she had felt for Zeke just twenty-four hours earlier.

"Come on, Sharpay," Zeke said, holding out his hand. "You owe me one."

"Well, all right," she said with a sigh. "After all, you *did* help with my rescue yesterday." As they walked towards the stage, she added hurriedly, "But let me take the lead, understand? You can sing background. *Softly.*"

He grinned and said, "Sure, whatever you say. You're the boss."

When the spotlight hit them, Sharpay launched into her song and Zeke dutifully stood behind her, crooning in the background. She saw Sammy dancing along from his spot by the audio equipment and watching her on stage. She smiled, seeing the look of adoration in his eyes. When she got to the second verse, Zeke stepped up next to her and took the microphone out of her hand. He began belting out the words with all the bravado of . . . well, of a true musical star!

Sharpay was so shocked, her mouth dropped. Then she noticed how everyone in the room was cheering. She glanced over at Zeke, who smiled at her and held out the mic so they could both sing into it.

She hesitated for just a moment. After all, she wasn't used to sharing the spotlight! But then she smiled back and leaned in towards Zeke. Together, they sang the next two verses with increasing spirit. During the last chorus, Zeke spun her around as she threw her head back and laughed. They ended with a flourish and then stood with their hands clasped, enjoying the sound of wild applause and cheering.

"That was a super performance!" the MC called out. "It's going to be hard to beat, but it's too early for the fun to stop . . . so who wants to try their luck next?"

As Sharpay ran down the steps to the dance floor, she felt as if she were floating on air. She hadn't been so happy since . . . well, she couldn't remember when she had felt this lighthearted. She even beamed at Troy and Gabriella as they brushed past her as they took the stage.

Then she spotted Sammy by the edge of the stage, giving her a thumbs-up. He pointed towards the speakers and mouthed the words,

"*Don't worry.*" Just to make the point clear, he drew one finger across his throat and gave her a knowing smile.

Sharpay suddenly remembered the scheme she had cooked up with Sammy! But now she felt so happy that she didn't want anyone's night to be ruined. Even Gabriella's.

She tried to push her way over to where Sammy was standing. She had to tell him that the plan was cancelled! But a group of people surged in front of her. By the time she fought her way over to where Sammy had been, he had vanished.

"And now we have Troy Bolton and Gabriella Montez, ready to try their luck!" the MC announced.

Sharpay saw the Wildcats cheering and closed her eyes in frustration. It was too late. Troy and Gabriella were about to sing. She'd never get to Sammy in time. . . .

The music started and Troy and Gabriella began to sing. Sharpay opened her eyes in surprise. She could hear every word, every note.

They had chosen a ballad. It started softly, then began to build in power. Sharpay looked at the audience. They were caught up in the moment, smiling as they sang.

She glanced at the stage. Troy and Gabriella were gazing into each other's eyes.

Sharpay felt a surge of hope that made her heart quicken. Maybe everything would be all right after all! Maybe . . . .

And then disaster hit, just as she and Sammy had planned. The lights went out, plunging the room into darkness. The music stopped in mid-note. Troy's and Gabriella's voices went silent.

Suddenly, people started to loudly complain and boo.

"Quiet, everybody! Let's stay calm!" Troy's voice rang out with authority and the room quickly settled down. "I'm sure this is just a momentary blackout," he continued.

The MC quickly stepped forward. "That's right," he said loudly. "I've just heard from the office. The lights have only gone out here in the club. So the staff members are coming in with candles and torches – ah, here they are!"

Several staff people came in carrying trays. On each tray, a dozen votive candles flickered with a warm, golden light. As the candles were placed around the room, the MC went on. "I'm sure the electricity will be back on soon. In the meantime–"

"In the meantime," Troy cut in quickly, "Gabriella and I would like to finish our per-formance."

The MC looked surprised. "Oh? You would?"

Troy gave Gabriella a questioning look. She smiled in response and said firmly, "Yes. We would."

By now the room was filled with candlelight. The soft light encouraged a hushed mood. There was a murmur of interest from the crowd as the MC said, "Very well. Once again – Troy Bolton and Gabriella Montez!"

"We were given this song yesterday by a

friend," Troy said. He winked at Ryan, who grinned. "It was written by another friend of ours, Kelsi Nielsen. Of course, it's not on the karaoke machine, but since the machine's not working right now—"

"We'd love to give it a try," Gabriella finished. She looked into Troy's eyes. He smiled at her. She smiled back and nodded slightly. Then he began to sing Kelsi's song.

Kelsi smiled from the audience; Jason gave her hand a proud squeeze.

After a few moments, Gabriella joined in. It was sweet. Simple. Heartfelt.

From her spot at the side of the stage, Sharpay watched and listened as the candlelight flickered over the faces in the audience. She knew, without a shred of doubt, that she had just lost the karaoke competition.

But, much to her surprise, she didn't care.

Thirty minutes later, the resort's electrician discovered the source of the power outage. It seemed that somehow the wires in the karaoke equipment had been mysteriously crossed, which had overloaded the circuits.

Sammy said he didn't know how it had happened, and promised to double check his work in the future.

Once the lights came on, however, everyone realized that Sammy's mistake had actually been a happy accident. The audience had decided to turn the lights back off and dance in the candlelit room.

"It's almost midnight," Troy said into Gabriella's ear. "Do you want to go outside to ring in the New Year?"

"That sounds perfect," she said, smiling up at him.

They stepped out onto the terrace. Gabriella glanced back through the windows. Silhouetted against the candlelight, she could see Taylor dancing with Chad, Ryan twirling Savannah around the floor, Kelsi talking and laughing with Jason . . . and Sharpay smiling at Zeke!

"I can't believe how much has changed in just one year," she murmured.

"That's true," Troy said. Gabriella turned back to look at him. A light snow had started to fall, and silver moonlight added a special touch. "But other things haven't changed at all. Here we are again, finishing, standing in the snow, waiting for the New Year, just like last year."

Gabriella could hear the countdown chant begin inside the club.

"Ten! Nine! Eight!"

Her mind flashed back twelve months. This time last year, she wouldn't have recognized this new Gabriella.

"Seven! Six! Five!"

A person with lots of good friends, and one in particular. A person who wasn't shy anymore, or not as much as she used to be. A person who was willing to try new things like singing on stage, even if she wasn't sure she could pull them off.

And all those changes had started in

this very spot.

"Four! Three! Two!"

She smiled, wondering what kind of changes the next year would bring.

"One! Happy New Year!"

Fireworks exploded in the sky and the sound of cheering erupted from the crowd inside.

"Happy New Year, Gabriella," Troy said.

"Happy New Year, Troy." She reached up and threw her arms around his neck.

Whatever the future held, she knew it would be sweet.

Something new is on the way!
Look for the next book in the Disney High
School Musical: Stories from East High series . . .

TURN UP THE HEAT

By Sarah Nathan
Based on the Disney Channel Original Movie
"High School Musical," Written by Peter Barsocchini
Based on "High School Musical 2," Written by Peter Barsocchini
Based on Characters Created by Peter Barsocchini

Gabriella Montez smiled as she walked down one of the long halls of East High. Leaning against her locker was the varsity basketball team captain, Troy Bolton. He waved at her as she walked towards him. This is the perfect way to start the day, she thought.

"Hey there!" Troy called as Gabriella got

closer. "I've been waiting for you. I made this for you." He held out a CD. He'd burned it the night before, after making what he'd hoped would be the perfect playlist. "The first song is by the band I was telling you about."

"Thanks," Gabriella said, touched that Troy had made her a CD. She reached out for the disc. "I can't wait to hear it!"

"Hear what?" Taylor McKessie asked, walking up behind Gabriella.

"Troy heard about this new band from his cousin. They're called 'The Cooks,'" Gabriella told her friend. She grinned at Troy, happy that he loved music as much as she did.

"Cool," Taylor said. "'The Cooks'? Does that CD come with any food? I was running late and didn't get to eat anything this morning."

"Hmm, I wish," Troy said, his stomach growling. "But these guys just cook up good music, not food."

"Luckily, I'm around, huh?" Zeke Baylor said, appearing before them. He had a large box in his hand. "I made these yesterday. Try one." He held out the open box filled with breakfast buns.

"Zeke!" Gabriella gushed. "You are the best!" She took a bite of the bun. Between the buttery, flaky crust and the sweet filling, the pastry melted in her mouth. "Yum," she added. "This is amazing."

Troy and Taylor each took a pastry, and then another hand swooped in.

"Can't miss a shot at a Zeke breakfast!" Chad Danforth cried. Then he took a huge bite.

"Did someone say Zeke brought breakfast?" Sharpay Evans asked from across the hall. She noticed that Zeke was holding open a box, and that usually meant that a delicious treat was inside. She waltzed over to stand next to him, peering into the box. "Hmm, what do you have there?"

"Oh, these?" Zeke said, trying to be casual. "I just whipped these up last night." He turned and offered Sharpay a closer look.

Gabriella watched as Sharpay carefully selected a pastry. It was no secret that Zeke had a crush on Sharpay. And, Gabriella mused, she was sure that Zeke made those pastries with the hope that Sharpay would have one. Sharpay liked the extra attention from Zeke – and the sweets that he gave her.

"Oh, *Zeke!*" Sharpay exclaimed, after she had taken a small bite. "This is simply *delicious*."

"Hey, Zeke," Troy said, licking his fingers. "That was really good."

Zeke didn't respond. He was staring straight ahead with his mouth hanging open and his eyes open extra wide. "He's . . . he's here," he finally managed to stutter, pointing down the hall.

His friends followed Zeke's finger and saw Principal Matsui walking towards them. Next to their principal was a tall man with jet-black hair, wearing jeans and a chocolate-brown leather jacket.

"Who's the dude with Principal Matsui?"

Chad asked. He eyed the man walking down the hall. "Nice jacket," he commented, nodding in approval at the man's cool-looking leather coat.

"Yes, who *is* that?" Sharpay asked, pushing Chad aside to get a better view of the good-looking man. "He looks like a movie star."

Zeke spun around to face his friends. "You don't know who that is?" he whispered. He couldn't believe that his friends had no idea who that man standing in the hallway was. Looking at their blank faces, he went on to explain, "That's Brett Lawrence – one of the best pastry chefs in the whole country. He's the host of *Bake-Off*!"

BRING IN THE NEW YEAR WITH EAST HIGH STYLE

The winter holidays are about spending time with the people you love, and thinking about the different ways you can make your lives even better next year. So that you have the best holiday, we've all tried to give you some ideas about how to make good New Year's resolutions, how to celebrate in style and our favourite winter sports and activities! Enjoy the holidays and have a happy New Year!

From everyone at East High! x

THE RIGHT RESOLUTIONS

Here's my advice on what makes a good New Year's resolution.

Remember that resolutions don't always have to be about yourself, try and think about how you can help your friends too.

Make sure you listen to your heart, be true to yourself and of course, be positive! A New Year means a fresh start and a new you.

LOOK OUT FOR YOUR FRIENDS

When Taylor and Chad tried to turn me and Troy away from each other, I felt terrible. But they soon realized that they should on our side. I'm going to try my best to look out for all my friends next year.

STAND UP FOR YOURSELF

I was too quick to turn away from my dream when I thought Troy wasn't interested in singing with me, but I should have been stronger and fought for what I believed in. So another resolution is make sure that I always stand up for myself in the future.

ACCEPT PEOPLE FOR WHO THEY ARE

Meeting new people is always hard. I found starting a new school difficult at first, but the key to making new friends is all about accepting people as they are. If you do this, then others will accept you in return.

Star Dazzle!

DON'T BE AFRAID TO ASK FOR HELP

I'm always under a lot of pressure at school. Sometimes I keep things bottled up inside. Next year I want to make a real effort to ask for help when I need it, whether it's from friends, family or teachers.

TRY TO THINK POSITIVELY

It can be really hard to stay positive when things go wrong. Next year I'm going to try my best to stay happy whatever the situation. I want to be an inspiration to my friends so that when they need me, I can be there for them and make them smile.

SHARPAY'S PERFECT OUTFIT

So now you have thought about your worthy New Year's resolutions. It's time to think about having some fun! What better way to start getting into the festive spirit than by picking the perfect party outfit?

Gabriella's Classic Look

This dress is stylish and chic, while still remaining simple and cute. Gabriella always manages to pull this look off. Although if you ask me she could do with a few more accessories and glitter.

Taylor's Smart & Casual

Taylor always looks smartly dressed, but funky too, thanks to some totally awesome accessories. Her hair looks fabulous, which means she's always got something to smile about.

SHARPAY'S SPANGLE

This is much more like it – how can you expect to be the life and soul of the party if you're not dressed to kill! Anything sparkly is perfect for the New Year's celebration.

Let's not forget about the boys! We need to make sure they look their best too!

TROY'S GOT TASTE

Don't you think Troy Bolton looks perfectly dressed for any occaision? He keeps it simple and clean – and anyone who dresses with his style is sure to have all the girls fighting over him at the party!

Chad's so cool

Although some people might accuse him of dressing down, there's a lot to be said for Chad's casual approach. He always looks ready for action, whether he's running down a basketball court or making moves on the dance floor.

ACE ACCESSORIES

I am SO the accessorizing queen, and I always knows how to look my best. Here are my top tips for making the best out of any outfit.

Decorate your head!
Hats aren't just for bad hair days you know – they're simply fabulous, as are any flowers or glittery hair slides you might want to decorate your hair with.

Bring along a bag!
You don't want your pockets bulging with phones, keys and wallets do you? Of course not. Make sure you have a stylish handbag that complements your outfit.

Enjoy your jewellery!
You could go without jewellery if you wanted to, but I always think that a sparkly neck is a beautiful neck! When the lights pick up the sparkle you'll look like a star!

SHARPAY'S BOYS' BEHAVIOUR GUIDE

As all fabulous young ladies know, it's important for the boys to act like perfect gentlemen, so here is my list of essentials for perfect party behaviour:

1. Try and make lots of eye contact with the person you're talking to (but not too much, or you'll just look like a crazy person).

2. Be a good listener. The last thing we like is some blabbermouth male who talks only about themselves. We want to know that you can listen too, you know!

3. Compliment your companion. We all like hearing that our outfits look great and that our hair and make-up is beautiful.

4. Offer to fetch us nibbles and drinks. If you're a real gentleman, you'll be attentive all evening and that'll score lots of good points with us!

5. Be sweet to our friends. What sort of a party is it if you stay hidden in the corner? We want to make sure everyone has fun, so get ready to show us a happy face!

WHAT'S YOUR PARTY PERSONA?

Go through the following questions and keep a note of your answers. Then check out the results at the end of the quiz to discover what your party persona is!

How do you usually get ready for a party?

A. You try on lots of different outfits and parade in front of the mirror until you find the perfect look.

B. You spend the afternoon worrying you won't have the courage to talk to anyone there.

C. You meet up with your friends so you can all get ready together.

What kind of outfit do you like to try and wear to a party?

A. As flashy, glittery and glamorous an outfit as possible – you like to stand out from the crowd!

B. You always try to dress down – it makes it easier to hide in the corner that way.

C. You'd wear your favourite outfit, because you know you feel comfortable AND look good!

What kind of entrance do you like to make?

A. You like to fling open the door and make sure everyone knows you've arrived!

B. You try and slide in behind another group, so no one stares at you.

C. You and your friends arrive together.

What kind of party do you enjoy the most?

A. Any party where you have the chance to shine, whether it's singing, dancing, or dazzling everyone with your wit and conversation.
B. A party where you can hide away in a corner if you want to.
C. You don't have a preference – you just like being able to be around other people having fun.

What are you like when you meet new people?

A. You are always entertaining and fabulous – new people flock to you.
B. You aren't very good at meeting new people and it makes you nervous.
C. You're always interested in meeting new people, and like getting to know them.

RESULTS!

IF YOU SCORED MOSTLY AS
You are the centre of attention! While it's true that people do flock to you, you might sometimes want to consider turning it down a little so that other people can have a chance to tell their stories too!

IF YOU SCORED MOSTLE BS
You shouldn't worry so much! People will like you for who you are, if you just have the courage to speak up and say "Hi" every now and then. Remember – neither Gabriella nor Troy wanted to sing that very first night at the party and just look what happened to them!

IF YOU SCORED MOSTLY CS
You seem to have a pretty good attitude about appropriate party behaviour and you'd make a fab party guest. You're kind and considerate of your friends, but always excited to meet new people too. Party on!

CHAD'S SNOWY SPORTS

I know from experience that not all sports come naturally. I was really worried about hitting the slopes, because the first time that I got on a snowboard, I kept falling over. It was only when my good friend, Troy, stepped in that I was able to get over my fear. Now I love boarding whenever I get a chance!

Boarding is the coolest winter sport. Just remember to follow the basic rules at all times and don't forget that you need to have professional lessons when you first start out!

Of course, some people always go for traditional skiing – there is something awesome about skiing down the mountain-side, and you can also go cross-country through some really amazing forests too.

WORDS EVERY BOARDER SHOULD KNOW

a 360
Spinning 360° while you are in the air.

face-plant
This is when you wipe out and fall face first into the snow!

Do an aerial
This means jumping high enough in the air that you get some space between the ground and the board!

airDog
An airdog is someone who's mostly interested in jumping tricks and spends most of their time in the air.

DRESS FOR SNOW-SPORTS SUCCESS

While some people might treat the ski slope like a fashion runway, you do need to think carefully about what to wear if you want to have fun!

GOOD GOGGLES

The sun can really hit the slopes hard and reflect off the snow, so you should try and get a really good pair of goggles to protect your eyes from the sun's rays.

SOLID SUNSCREEN

The sun's rays reflecting off the snow can also damage your skin, so it's important to apply lots of sunscreen throughout the day!

WATERPROOF LAYER

If doesn't matter how fashionable you are — you'll be freezing if you don't make sure your outside layers are waterproof. Even the best boarders need a break from the action and it won't be much fun if your clothes get soaked!

TIME TO BE SEEN!

Last but not least, even the most trendsetting skiers wear bright clothes so that they can be seen by everyone on the slopes.

HOW ABOUT A LITTLE APRÈS SKI?

Of course, you don't need to hit the slopes to have a great winter holiday! There are plenty of other ways to enjoy the cold weather, if you want a day off from the top of the mountain action!

SKATING

Even if you're not lucky enough to go to an outdoor skating rink, there are plenty of indoor ones where you can fly around to your heart's content – just be careful not to wipe anyone out as you go!

SNOWBALL FIGHTS

Some may say they're a little childish, but I still think you can't beat a good old fashioned snowball fight! You need tactics, teams and a good strategy if you want to win – you gotta get'cha head in the game!

SNOW ANGELS

You wouldn't catch me making snow angels, but I know some of the other guys like them. I guess it's kinda fun, lying on your back in the snow. Maybe I could make a snow basketball player instead?

CURLING UP BY THE FIRE

You've seen Gabriella curling up with a good book. I guess it can be cool to sit close to a fire and get all warmed up, but only after you've spent the day on the mountain first!

WHAT DO YOUR SPORTS SAY ABOUT YOU?

Go through the following questions and keep a note of your answers. Then check out the results at the end of the quiz to find your favourite winter sports!

What's your favourite way to get down the slopes?

A. You like to shoot down on your skis.
B. You like to carve your way down on a slammin' board!
C. You like to stay on the chair lift and get back down that way.

There are three different slopes to choose from – which do you take?

A. You take the widest slope with the most people around to show off to
B. You take the hardest, steepest slope you can find – you like the thrill!
C. You take the gentlest slope you can find, one that's really easy!

Which of these winter's evening activities do you prefer?

A. You like to pamper yourself and relax in the sauna.
B. You want to go to a kickin' party!
C. You enjoy reading quietly by the fire.

Snow angels – what do you say?

A. They're kind of fun, but you'd be too embarrassed to make one in public!
B. Definitely! Especially if you were with the right crowd.
C. Absolutely not – they're just for kids.

How do you feel at the end of a winter holiday?

A. Exhausted and totally ready to restart your fabulous life at home.
B. The holiday's never long enough – if you could only have one more day on the slopes!
C. Relieved – you hate being put under pressure to do so many sporty things all the time!

RESULTS!

IF YOU SCORED MOSTLY AS
Although winter sports may not be your greatest love in life, you're great at joining in activities and you feel pretty happy strutting your stuff on the slopes.

IF YOU SCORED MOSTLY BS
Wow – it's hard to keep you off the mountain! Once you're up there you never want to come down!

IF YOU SCORED MOSTLY CS
On the whole, you're happiest snuggling up near the fire in the lodge than you are halfway up a mountain. But remember there's a lot of fun to be had in the snow, if you're ready to learn how to have it!

EAST HIGH RESOLUTIONS

Gabriella
I'm going to try and think more positively and make my friends happy, while still being true to myself.

TROY
I'm going to stand up for myself, and never, ever give up on a dream.

TAYLOR
I'm going to make sure I accept people for who they are and really listen to my friends, especially when they need my help.

CHAD
I'm going to support my friends and accept that everyone's different, but that's what makes us all so great!

SHARPAY
I'm going to try and accessorize better. That's okay, isn't it?

What will your resolutions be this New Year?